Praise for Emily Franklin's
The Principles of Love **novels**

"F

"L
wr

"A
tin

"V
at
an

"\

"I
ch
he
al
F

"Both funny and moving, *The Principles of Love* is a wild ride that gives a fresh perspective on what really goes on at boarding school. I couldn't help but get sucked into Love Bukowski's life, and look forward to her next adventures."

—Angie Day, producer of MTV's *Made*
and author of *The Way to Somewhere*

"Whether you're sixteen and looking forward or thirty-six and looking back, the first book in the Love Bukowski series will pull your heartstrings with comic, poignant, and perceptive takes on the teenage tribulations of lust, life, and long-lost mothers."

—Heather Swain, author of *Luscious Lemon*
and *Eliot's Banana*

"It's easy to fall in love with Love Bukowski. Emily Franklin's novel is fun, funny, and wise—a great book for readers of all ages." —M. E. Rabb, author of *The Rose Queen*
and the Missing Persons mystery series

Also by Emily Franklin

The Principles of Love
Piece, Love, and Happiness
Love from London
All You Need Is Love

the PRINCIPLES of L♥VE

Summer of Love

Emily Franklin

nal
Jam
books

NAL Jam
Published by New American Library, a division of Penguin Group (USA) Inc., 375 Hudson Street, New York, New York 10014, USA • Penguin Group (Canada), 90 Eglinton Avenue East, Suite 700, Toronto, Ontario M4P 2Y3, Canada (a division of Pearson Penguin Canada Inc.) • Penguin Books Ltd., 80 Strand, London WC2R 0RL, England • Penguin Ireland, 25 St. Stephen's Green, Dublin 2, Ireland (a division of Penguin Books Ltd.) • Penguin Group (Australia), 250 Camberwell Road, Camberwell, Victoria 3124, Australia (a division of Pearson Australia Group Pty. Ltd.) • Penguin Books India Pvt. Ltd., 11 Community Centre, Panchsheel Park, New Delhi - 110 017, India • Penguin Group (NZ), 67 Apollo Drive, Mairangi Bay, Auckland 1311, New Zealand (a division of Pearson New Zealand Ltd.) • Penguin Books (South Africa) (Pty.) Ltd., 24 Sturdee Avenue, Rosebank, Johannesburg 2196, South Africa

Penguin Books Ltd., Registered Offices:
80 Strand, London WC2R 0RL, England

First published by NAL Jam, an imprint of New American Library,
a division of Penguin Group (USA) Inc.

First Printing, March 2007
10 9 8 7 6 5 4 3 2 1

Copyright © Emily Franklin, 2007
All rights reserved

NAL JAM and logo are trademarks of Penguin Group (USA) Inc.

LIBRARY OF CONGRESS CATALOGING-IN-PUBLICATION DATA:
Franklin, Emily.
Summer of love / Emily Franklin.
p. cm.—(Principles of love)
Summary: After a difficult junior year at Hadley Hall, Love looks forward to a carefree summer on Martha's Vineyard running her late Aunt Mable's cafe with her best friend Arabella but the clues about Love's family history that her aunt has left for her to find and piece together bring some surprising and troubling revelations.
ISBN: 978-0-451-22040-0
ISBN-10: 0-451-22040-4
[1. Coming of age—Fiction. 2. Family—Fiction. 3. Interpersonal relations—Fiction. 4. Summer—Fiction. 5. Martha's Vineyard (Mass.)—Fiction.] I. Title.
PZ7.F8583Sum 2007
[Fic]—dc22   2006026368

Set in Bembo • Designed by Elke Sigal

Printed in the United States of America

For Nicole and that summer,
that car, that song; sixteen going on seventeen

Summer of Love

Chapter 1

There's nothing like the feeling of waking up next to the guy who got first dibs on your heart. Even if, as you open your eyes, you realize your hair is wet with the dew from sleeping outside on someone's lawn and your whole body aches with the remnants of last night's festivities.

Wait. Back up. I open my eyes to the first rays of morning light that hover and wave above the horizon line at Crescent Beach. *The* Crescent Beach—the site of many a hookup and heartbreak, many a heave and a ho (bag), the place all Hadley students go to celebrate the trek through yet another academic year's ending.

After a last-minute decision (which in itself is a break in character for me; I mean, I'm not the most spontaneous person in the world) not to head right to Martha's Vineyard, where my summer java job and best friend, Arabella, are waiting for me, I rerouted and revamped and re-everythinged to get here. Here being the grassy patch of hill that overlooks the sandy beach that is strewn with bits of revelry: beer cans and sweatshirts, discarded boxes of graham crackers and blobs of half-eaten marshmallows left over from the three a.m. attempt at making s'mores. All along the beach and grass are sleeping bag–covered bodies, couples (old, new, and YECs—year-end couples that start at the prom and last through the end-of-the-year parties to assure that you'll have someone to smooch by the bonfires), and—amidst all this debris—me.

I'm lying on my back looking at the wide, misty sky. It's the kind of morning that starts off chilly and misty and then—suddenly—breaks into a hot, sunny day. But right now, I'm tucked into my red sleeping bag. It's lined with plaid flannel and since I'm sock and shoeless, I can feel the worn material on my toes and I close my eyes again. Moments later, when I turn my head to the right and open them, I am looking at Jacob. Jacob with whom I already have a rather long history of liking, losing, and—most recently—being *friends in quotes* with (the kind of person you're friends with but that requires an explanation every time you think about them or bring them up in conversation).

So Jacob is on his back and I'm on mine and we both have our heads turned in, so we're facing each other. It's like nothing else exists except us and the soft sound of waves on the shore.

"Hey," Jacob whispers to me, his green eyes still half sleep-closed, his face just a bit stubbly, his dark curls slightly ruffled.

"Hey back," I say, since it feels appropriate to sound familiar since we're both on our backs next to each other.

"Last night was . . ." He starts and then stops, looking up at the empty sky above us.

"Insert adjective here: (a) fun (b) clichéd (c) a combination of the two."

"I'll take C for five hundred," he says.

"You're totally mixing game shows here," I say, and he rolls his head back so we're looking at each other again. In some ways it's like I'm back a whole year to the same Crescent Beach party where Jacob and I broke up, even though then we were sophomores and now we've just finished junior year and senior year looms three months away.

"Give me a break; it's not even six in the morning," he says with a grin. Then he switches gears. "Hey, do you remember trying to eat a s'more with no hands last night?"

I nod. "Didn't you get marshmallow in your hair?"

"Yeah. Some girl cut off a piece—it was so tangled," he says.

"That girl will probably try and sell it on eBay or some-thing—you being such a campus rock star and all," I say, giv-ing him a hard time for no reason at all except that we're alone and I've been trying to deal with the fact that while I was away in London last term, he was morphing from unnoticed cam-pus quiet boy into Hadley hunk (even though I despise that word—it's so retro I can't even think about bringing it back—and yet . . .)

"It's not that bad, Love," Jacob says and keeps looking me. "Is it?"

I twist my mouth up and raise my eyebrows. "I don't know. It depends on who you want to be on campus, I guess."

"I just want to be myself," he says and then sticks his tongue out. "Could I sound more pathetic?"

"It was kind of like a bad rock anthem—*I wanna be myself by JC*," I say in a DJ voice. For a millisecond I let myself fantasize about my potential voice-over gig in L.A. this summer. (Courtesy of Martin Gregory Eisenstein, the indie film producer who just happened to invite me to his annual posh gala, btw, my mom's name, on July third; he gave me the code word to gain entrance—Mercury—but how I'd get out there is a mystery . . . like many things in my life—including my mother, whose name I know but whose presence in my life up till now has been nil. But now I'm officially digressing to the point of an out-of-body experience.) I look at Jacob and am sucked back into the here and now. The here and now-kiss-me-please-please-please.

But we're just quiet and looking at each other while still lying flat on our backs. I can't see what's to his right and to my left are just sandy dunes and sea grass. Near perfection. Well, except for the fact that I don't know what all this means. Last night is really a blur of beer and music, tearful girls getting overemotional when certain songs came over the outdoor speakers, guys I've never noticed before suddenly being super-friendly, thanks to a couple of shots.

"Is it my weird imagination or did people skinny-dip while singing 'It's a Small World'?" Jacob asks. "The details of last night are—um—a little fuzzy."

I laugh quietly and nod. "It's one of those party scenes that makes total sense at the time, but when you remember it later it's like, *Why were we singing that? And what was so appealing about getting naked in the frigid Atlantic?*"

"I don't seem to recall any nakedness on your part," Jacob says. I can hear rustling. In the distance a car engine starts—probably someone making a run to Dunkin' Donuts to buy coffee and munchkins for the masses. Whoever that is, I bless them.

"Nope, not so much into the bare-ass buck-naked ocean thing," I say and then wonder if it sounds like I'm a prude or judgmental, so I add, "I mean, I'd get into it with the right person, but . . ."

There's a distinct possibility, I realize suddenly, that Jacob (a) could be that person and (b) could kiss me—morning breath, matted hair, and all—right now. He moves his head a little closer to me and whispers, "Listen, as long as we're on the subject of nakedness and such . . ."

I love that he can pull off using awkward expressions like *and such*. I love that he looks so cute even after only a few hours of sleep. I love how he looks at me so long it seems like he's studying me, trying to memorize all of me before we part ways for the summer. I love how I'm just so fickle and even though I semirecently got dumped on my ass by Arabella's hot Brit-boy brother, Asher, I can easily be distracted by another pretty face. Except that Jacob Coleman is much more than a pretty face. He's got a pretty bod, too. No—he's got enough brains and quirks to balance out his physical presence.

"Yeah?" I ask and prepare for my kiss by making sure my lips aren't flaky but aren't too moist either. (Note to self: Moist is a gross word.)

"So you know how I went to Logan Airport to—"

"I remember. Didn't you go get your mom?" I ask and

angle my head so it will be easy for Jacob to lean in, to do that thing where the guy props his forearm and palm on the ground and leans down to—

"It wasn't my mother," Jacob says and nudges me. I assume he means for me to snuggle into him, so I wriggle a little way out of the warm cocoon of my sleeping bag and nearer to his chest. Yum. Jacob raises his eyebrows in surprise but doesn't mind. In fact, he reaches over and brushes my red hair so it's out of my face and then nudges me again. "It wasn't my mother," he repeats and when he nudges me a third time, I sit up for the first time since I woke up. There, lying on his right, this whole time, is . . .

I make a face—I can't help it. I try to just remain blank, but the person next to Jacob, still slumbering soundly, is everything I'm not, at least physically. I study her for a second—tree-limbed and perfectly pale with that hint of blush on her cheeks, Sleeping Beauty's hair is cascading down around her shoulders, elegantly messy—and her stunning jawline and flawless face are visible from underneath said hair spillage (sandy blond, no roots, no visible highlights). I lie back and feel like I got kicked in the stomach with a riding boot. Not that I personally know how that would feel, but Arabella—who actually owns her own horse—has relayed the info to me and it sounds gut-wrenching. Like now. Asher cheated on me with some cutting-edge artist named Valentine (could he not segue into a normal name after mine? The similarity is revolting even to me) and now Jacob—wait. No. He didn't cheat on me. We weren't together, not at all. And yet it sort of feels the same way. I guess if you have feelings (hidden or exposed) for someone and they don't return the sentiments but then hitch on to someone else, you can still feel betrayed.

Suddenly the morning seems different. I went to a lame party last night, didn't partake in the skinny-dipping, didn't get kissed, missed my ferry for Martha's Vineyard, and my dear Aunt Mable—who passed away only recently—is exactly who I want to tell all of this to, but I can't.

"Sorry," Jacob says, his voice just slightly above a whisper. Sleeping Beauty stirs next to him.

I get pre-bitchy. "For what? You have nothing to be sorry about," I say, even though I don't believe it.

"Her name is Juliette," he says.

"Of course it is," I say and sigh.

"We met when I was studying in Switzerland and we'd planned this visit and . . ." Jacob tries to rake his hands through his hair, sitting up and looking at both of us—me and Juliette. (He pronounces it the French way, *Juuoolietah*. Bite me.) "And I kind of got the feeling that you thought I was getting my mom at Logan and . . ."

I sit up and slide out of my sleeping bag. My feet are wet on the green dewy grass and I am seriously in need of coffee and comfort food. Can you say omelet? Or, in French, *omelette*? I begin to roll up my sleeping bag, trying to keep my voice down so as not to wake Harriet Walters, who is curled up with her jocky boy of late, Welsh, whose snores are louder than the waves. "Why didn't you want to correct me, then, if you knew I thought you were getting your mom and not Juliette?" I ask and do him the courtesy of pronouncing it his way even though I want to do it the regular way.

Jacob shakes his head and closes his mouth, looking away from me and focusing instead on the ocean. "I'm not sure. That's something I'm still trying to work out . . ."

I stand up with my rolled-up sleeping bag tucked under one arm and my pride tucked away so as not be wounded further. It's not that I thought Jacob wanted me—okay, maybe a little—it's more that last night, when I just followed a whim and drove up here, I felt carefree, something I haven't felt in a long time. And being around Jacob highlighted that—like he brings out parts of me that are otherwise shy. But now that I see the foreign girlfriend, I remember she was around last night—only I chose not to notice her, figuring that she was someone's friend from another prep school. But I guess I was wrong. And I guess even though it's easy to imagine sliding from *friends with quotes* to couple, it's just not going to happen. And the friendship part is murky at best.

"I should go," I say and stand there waiting for Jacob to do something.

He looks at the ground and then puts his warm hand on my bare foot, leaving it there while he says, "Are you mad?"

I shake my head. It's impossible to get angry with him because he didn't do anything. I didn't do anything. And maybe that's part of the problem—we're so busy *not* doing anything that nothing's happening. "Not mad, just ready for summer," I say.

Jacob keeps his hand on my foot until Juliette sits up suddenly, rubs her eyes like a heroine in a Disney movie, and says,

"Bon matin" in a way that's seductive enough that even the beach wants to do her. Jacob removes his hand from my foot and I remove myself from the post-party scene.

"Bye, Jacob," I say. "Or, um, *au revoir.*" It's French and means, literally, *see you again*, which, of course, I will in the fall, three months from now when the summer is all in memory form but which right now is waiting for me to discover. Jacob starts to say something to me but is distracted by his visiting vixen, so I just shove my sleeping bag into my already-filled car. Rather than risk losing my keys (good thing I didn't lose anything else, as many a Hadley girl has at these post-graduation frolics) I had left them in the glove compartment of my car, so I pinch the little lock open and find them. Also in the compartment is a pamphlet from Mrs. Dandy-Patinko, my college counselor. (Just the thought of TCP—the college process—is enough to dampen even the sunniest of mornings, which this isn't yet.)

Standing on the gravel drive with the little pebbles digging into my winterized feet (they haven't yet built up that thick summer skin—and neither, I guess, has my heart. Is that poignant or just a bad rock lyric?) I hold the flyer—it details Mrs. Dandy-Patinko's brother's pottery place, a Vineyard establishment I hope to visit. All of this tempts me to tear into the package Aunt Mable left for me, but I know I can't. She worked hard to leave behind articles and words in which I could find solace after her death and I have to admit that knowing there's a package with a mysterious treasure in it does help. Her ex-fiancé, Miles, helped to get all of the contents of said package ready and his specific instructions from Mable were "to let my summer unfold." I assume (then again, I have a habit of putting the ass back in assume) she meant that it's best to just let things happens, not to try to control or determine. But she also knows I'm not the most laissez-faire person in the world and that leaving things to chance gives me emotional hives.

So. My summer should unfold. I'm holding the pottery pamphlet while I'm thinking this and suddenly it dawns on me that since Mrs. Dandy-Patinko gave me this bit of potentially touristy trash, I've yet to open it. I perch on the passenger seat next to Jim. Jim being my giant overstuffed hiking pack. I named him because he is my traveling companion and actually a fairly decent boyfriend so far—no musical tastes on which to disagree, no stinky feet or bad breath, no wandering eye. The fact that he's Gore-Tex is only a slight problem. But I digress.

Looking at the brochure, it seems obvious that I should have at least done Mrs. Dandy-Patinko the courtesy of scanning the info—after all, she's guiding me toward the next four years of my life and all she wanted me to do was look up her aging, throwback-to-another-era (her words, not mine) brother. The front depicts a bearded man in clay-splattered overalls working seriously at a pottery wheel. Nothing super-exciting there. But then, when I open it—or, um, *unfold* the pamphlet—Aunt Mable's familiar print-script is there.

> Took you long enough! For someone who's so into other
> people's stories, I knew you'd wait to unfold this. Now

that you've taken the first step, the next is to visit
Tink (not the fairy in Peter Pan). If you relax and let
summer come to you instead of running after it, you'll
enjoy it more. Let your cup runneth over, as they say.
(Who the hell they are, I don't know—but it sounds
validating, doesn't it?)

The tears never leave my eyes—yes, my eyes well up, but
they don't spill over. It's like Mable knows—knew—me so
well, she knew what my reaction would be and I'm appreciative of her insights. But Tink? I'm confused for all of three seconds until I flip to the other side of the page and find Watson
Patinko's address c/o Menemsha Potters. Patinko = Tink. Got
it. I am my own detective! Mable and I once joked about becoming private eyes—not in the gruesome televised way, but
in the film noir, black stockings, tweed suits, dramatic music
way. Now I'm kind of getting to do that. Except barefoot.

I stand up, strap Jim in (fake boyfriend or not, I'll keep him
safe on the road), and feel totally ready to leave behind Crescent Beach, Hadley Hall people, and another night's assumptions. I rummage around for my flip-flops.

Of course, I find two flip-flops, but they don't match. One
is black-soled with orange strappy things (or whatever you call
the toe parts of flip-flops) and one is from an old outing with
Aunt Mable, black with a red fake flower in the middle. At least
they are right and left footed, so I slide them on and drive,
aware that when I walk around with these shoes, it will look
like I'm making a statement about myself. Either I'm artsy and

different, or dorky and disheveled, but no one will know just by looking that I didn't brush my teeth the night before, that I believe it's possible to like the Clash singing "Spanish Bombs" and Madonna's "Borderline" equally, that my car is crammed with summer stuff for my job at Slave to the Grind II (Mable's soon-to-be-renamed café), and that I am actively forgetting a boy named Jacob and actively seeking summer distractions. Or, as Arabella likes to call them, SFs: summer friends, summer flings, summer . . . whatevers. I'm supposed to relax and let summer find me, right? Then again, what can you tell about people by their exteriors, their school sweatshirts, their houses, their mismatching shoes?

Chapter 2

In order to bring my car to Martha's Vineyard, I had to get reservations months ago. And in choosing to go to Crescent Beach yesterday, I lost my spot. So now I'm faced with that ever-adult issue of taking responsibility for my own actions (read: pleading with the ticket people to get me on a boat now).

"You can go standby," the ticket guy says from behind the safety of the glass wall. Clearly the people who design ticket booths must know that irate customers need the barrier.

"But I have to get there today. Like, now," I say and then hate myself for saying *like*. It only makes me sound more petty and annoying and it doesn't get me any closer to the island, where my job, friend, and life await my arrival.

"I understand what you're saying," Ticket Master says and checks something on the computer screen to make it seem like he's got many more issues to take care of other than my little mishap. "But the fact is you gave up your space."

"But I called. I asked about trading . . ."

"This is a ferry operation, not a baseball card swap," he says, weary of me and my whining. "Here." He hands me a slip of paper.

"What's this?"

"It's the standby ticket. Go back to your car, ask the parking lot attendant where to go, and get in line."

"Will I be on the next ferry?" I ask, clutching the piece of paper like it's the Wonka Golden Ticket.

"You'll be lucky to get there by dusk," he says and directs me out the door.

Two hours and three ferries later, I'm pulling an album cover stance (knees bent, hair down, tank top and sunglasses on) and sitting on the hood of my crumbly, rusting Saab and debating the merits of hot dog versus just onion rings, while people-watching and trying not to get burned. As predicted, the sun came out full blast right when I got in line and—since you can't leave your car and my a/c is broken (or correction, never worked in the first place)—I am slowly turning shades of pink.

"You are in so much trouble," says the voice on the other end of my cell phone. Thankfully, the voice belongs to English and energetic Arabella Piece, who is kidding. "Don't worry—I covered for you. It meant I worked a double shift, but when you didn't show up I figured there must be a really good reason."

"Well, thanks, Bels—I owe you one," I say and hop down from the hood to look for some SPF for my face and arms.

"So," she says, "give me the dirt. What's so important that you had to miss your ferry and your first day of work?"

I shake my head like she can see me. "Nothing. It turns out—nothing."

"Thank you for that electrifying and informative debriefing . . . Now, speaking of debriefing . . ."

"Oh, God, Arabella, what'd you do now?" I ask and smile.

Arabella laughs. "I'm tossing my hair around and giggling into the mirror like I'm at a press conference," she says. "But like I'd say to the media—no comment."

"So you're not going to tell me anything?" I ask and wonder what—or whom—Arabella is doing across the bay.

"Let's just put it this way: If you want a summer fling, you'll definitely get one," she says. "I might just have a couple. Oh—and Chris called here since he couldn't reach you on your cell phone."

"Is he okay?" I look at my phone and pat it like it's a puppy. "There was no reception at Crescent Beach." And not much of anything else, I might add.

"He's fine—I think—but he said he has a change of plans."

"Oh, how mysterious . . ." I say and wish Chris were here to add levity and grace to my day. But Chris isn't here. He's on his way to visit his first real boyfriend, Alistair, who will probably turn out to be perfect. And Chris deserves that. But I wish they could have their romance closer to the East Coast. Then he and I could hang out with Chili Pomroy—the ultra-hip soon-to-be-Hadley student, who of course summers on the Vineyard with her artist-scene parents. "Have you seen Chili? She only got there last night, but she was going to drop by the café."

"No—not yet. But I'm breathless with anticipation," Arabella cracks. She doesn't so much have an issue with Chili, but I think she resents the idea of someone else taking up my time. It's like even the bounds of friendship are tested by time suckage—jobs, guys, other friends—we'll have to see how it all pans out. Arabella coughs and lets the words rush out of her mouth. "Now, I have to run. Henry's helping me finish some things here and then we're going out to lunch with Tyler, Jason, Lissa, Jay Daventree, and that lot."

I remember Henry's preppy posse vaguely, but it's odd that Arabella is so entrenched in Vineyard life already and I'm not even there yet.

"So you're not at Henry's now?" I ask. From our conversations a while ago I thought Arabella had taken up residence at Henry Randall's quaint seaside mansion.

"I was, but I'm not now, no. We're—I'm—at the flat above the café—our place. Yours and mine. See you soon!"

"Who's there with you?" I ask, but Arabella's already clicked off, being the quick hanger upper that she is. Of course she could be alone or she could have some summer fling there or she could have gotten together with Henry. And would that be a problem? I think about this as the next ferry comes in, sounds its low whistle, boards cars (not mine) and people (not me) and leaves.

Arabella could date Henry—it's not like I ever did or really wanted to. But maybe I do like him—or could. Or maybe I'm romantically challenged. If I'm really honest, Henry has lurked in the background as sort of a backup guy.

Not in a mean way, like I know I could have him and I'll just string him along, but more like he's sweet and steady and there's pretty much a clean slate there (save for him thinking I'm older than I really am. As Dad says, one lie breeds another. Henry assumed I was an undergrad at Brown University and I never bothered to correct him. Just like Jacob did with me and his "visitor"). Anyway, even though there have been no romantic overtures from Henry or from me toward him, I guess the truth is I'm not so psyched about anyone else dating him either. Including Arabella.

"You—black Saab—you're on, go!" the parking attendant shouts at me and waves me into the line of cars moving toward the gaping mouth of the ferry. I quickly jump in, start my engine, and go slowly up the ramp and onto the boat that will carry me toward my summer.

The cars are all parked in lines on the lowest level of the ferry boat and after I've locked up, I climb the metal staircase to the next level, then another flight until I'm on the top deck. The snack bar line is too long to contend with, so I take my lukewarm fizzy water (I am slowly developing an addiction to the carbonation) outside.

Rows of blue plastic chairs are bolted to the deck and passengers lounge with their canvas tote bags (some monogrammed, others plain) while seagulls careen and dive for food and little kids run around shrieking. A nice June scene. Sipping the tepid liquid, I make a quick call to my dad, leaving a message that lets him know I'm alive and well and Vineyard bound. It's a shame to ruin the tranquillity (if you can call screeches from the gulls and loud, whiny toddlers tranquil) with my phone, but daughterly responsibility is something I keep in mind—even more so now because my dad has made the brilliant decision that I should board at Hadley this fall rather than live in my quasi–day student life at home on campus.

But this, and college, and everything else are fading into the distance as the mainland recedes and the island is nearly in view. It's amazing to think that such a small piece of land can hold so much for me. I go to the railing and squint to see the houses that dot the outskirts of the island. Gray-shingled massive mansions that are casually referred to as cottages, sweet Victorian houses painted bright colors, a lighthouse, and lots of buoys and moorings and fishing boats. Possibly, Charlie is on one of these. Possibly, he could think of me from time to time—or possibly, I am dreaming. Plus, even though Charlie is without a doubt one of the hottest people ever to walk the planet (or crawl) he is also a guy who lured me in, got me hooked (just to really play up the fishing imagery, since he is in fact a fisherman), and left me beached (okay, that's maybe too whalelike). So we had one fun night together last fall. So he's obviously a smart guy with a clever wit. So I recently saw him again in Harvard Square (a sighting for which I have no explanation). So I then bumped into him again by the ferry and he was nice. And still hot. It doesn't mean anything.

It doesn't mean anything except that I am hoping to (hoping = counting on) bump into him again at some point.

Of course, *some point* to me means maybe this week or in the first few weeks I'm on the Vineyard. Not, like the reality, as I'm walking back to my car. The mumbly voice on the speaker announced that passengers who drove need to go back to their cars, so, like the licensed lemming I am, I follow all of the passengers and their totes and toddlers back down the metal steps toward the car level and only then do I spot Charlie and his truck.

Okay—I never really pictured myself as a girl who would be drawn to a guy with a pickup, but then again, maybe that's because I don't live in Texas or someplace where owning trucks or driving them is standard. At prep school, everyone's carless. And even though some of the kids I go to school with own fancy cars already, or have a chauffeur, the Vineyard scene is much lower key. Famous people and their flocks, old money and their minions, drive beat-up old Jeeps from the late seventies or walk around in faded jeans or khakis fraying at the hems. It's the worn-in rich look—like I'm so moneyed or cultured I don't need a label or outfit to prove otherwise. That said, Charlie's truck is clearly a working truck, not a rich-kid hand-me-down, and his fishing gear and various tools in the back are all roped down.

My heart races as I debate saying hello or hiding in my car. I want to bump into him, but I want to bump into him when I look decent or at least have showered off the sludge and sand and party remains from last night. So basically the ideal situation would be to bump into him when I'm already dressed to go out elsewhere—like Arabella and I are walking down Main

Street heading to meet Henry and his friends. Yeah, like that. But since I can't create the bump into, I decide I'll go over and say hi now. Besides, he's probably not interested in me and he's the only person I've ever had stand me up—so.

So I walk over, sucking in my stomach to squeeze through the miniscule spaces between vehicles, and manage to bonk myself with only one side mirror and one bumper as I try to cross over into the line where Charlie's truck is parked near a metal post. I get to the side of the truck and slow my stride. Sure, we're about to dock and yes, I've got to get back to my car, but I walk past the cab and put my hand on the driver's side window to say hello.

"Hi," I say in a bland but friendly way so that Charlie can do nothing but interpret my greeting as an island hello.

"Ah, hi," says the hippie-chic girl in the passenger seat. "How's it going?"

I stammer and then manage, "Good." I can't help but stare at her. She's got turquoise earrings and a deep tan that make me think of an Eagles song Mable used to sing: *I like the way your sparkling earrings lay against your skin so brown* . . . But anyway, earth to Love.

"Are you looking for Charlie?" Hippie asks, somehow able to make a threadbare faded red T-shirt seem as elegant as an evening gown. Note to self: Must shower and attempt cleanliness.

I nod and the loudspeaker announces we're pulling into port. I need to go before I get caught in the rush of traffic. "Yeah."

She smiles, revealing her perfectly white teeth, and stretches her bare feet (also tan) out the window, the essence of summer casual cool. "He went to get us something to drink."

Us. Right. "Oh, well, I have to get back to my car, but I'll . . ." My voice gets lost in the hum of engines starting up and the ferry horn blasting. Hippie Girl nods and gives some weird wave, maybe an island peace symbol or something befitting her gauzy Indian-print vibe, and I walk away feeling dorky and disillusioned.

Why I thought Charlie was single is a mystery. The best answer I can give is because I want him to be. Just like I see Henry as a potential in the background even though he's never said anything to give me that impression. All my views are filtered through my brain and therefore are twisted to suit my own desires. And where does this leave me now?

Driving off the boat with my windows rolled down, breathing in the salty air, my shoulders immediately relaxing into a summer slouch. After I pull out of the driveway and onto the road, I stop at the intersection and try to pick which way to turn. Moments like this either fly by unnoticed or feel weighty—like if you pick one way one thing will happen and if you pick the other, your whole life could be different. But maybe it's just an intersection and nothing more. I signal left and then notice Charlie's red pickup truck ahead turning right, going up the hill past Vineyard Haven, and wonder whether I should drive right to the café or follow that red pickup truck just a little ways around the island, to see where it (and by it I mean Charlie and his hippie lady) leads me.

Option two wins out and I flip my directional and go right, hanging back like the true private detective that I am. The roads on Martha's Vineyard are all looped and connected—eventually every street leads to every town—so I don't feel like a stalker, just, um, a very enthusiastic tourist. Through the wooded area, past the Black Dog bakery, past a miniature golf course where I have to insist on taking Arabella (who thinks she's such a natural putter that if the acting thing doesn't work out she might putt professionally), and then I let the truck go ahead, off in the distance as the woods give way to clear fields and marsh.

When we (and by we I mean me and my sad sleuthing self) get to Menemsha, Charlie and his luscious lady (I can still see her perfect feet sticking out the window) pull over to the right on a sandy, dusty road and I wait until I can't hear or see the truck before proceeding. Inching the car up without stalling, I stop by the foot of the driveway to see where the truck has gone. Parked by a small shingled cottage (a real cottage, not a mansion cottage), I can see Charlie emerge from the driver's side, and watch him walk around to Hippie's door and virtually lift her out—maiden in distress that she is. So this is their cozy summer shack. They walk up the steps of the porch to go inside and do God-knows-what while I feel jealous and then annoyed at my jealousy. One: I never really had Charlie, and two: If Hippie wants to be with a guy who strands you at a diner, then she can have him. I, however, am on the road to bigger and better things.

I figure since I'm in Menemsha and already semilost, I may

as well try and find Menemsha Potters, where Mrs. Dandy-Patinko's brother lives. And pots. *What an odd verb*, I think as I circle around a wooded cove and past a couple of beachy stores. Then a very helpful signpost appears in front of the general store. It's one of those signs that have town names and stores painted onto individual wooded planks that jut off in all directions—Edgartown, where I'm supposed to be right now, that way; beach, that way; post office, over there; Hale Farm, that way, and—yes—Menemsha Potters, one half mile to the left.

A blue and red faded sign in the shape of a big mug swings from a post at the edge of the road and I turn onto the sand and dirt drive, following it past a couple of oversized bulls (maybe they are regular sized, but they are enormous enough to warrant the supersize name) and a crumbling little house, and park my car in front of a large barn.

In front of the barn are shelves piled with ceramic bowls, pitchers, and chowder mugs. I carry the pamphlet from Aunt Mable with me like it's a ticket of admission—welcome to the show of my summer—and stop to admire the pottery as I go by. The coffee mugs are perfect; round bowled at the bottom with a small neck so they won't slosh on you. Too good to pass up—what kind of seventeen-year-old am I that I am more captivated by a coffee cup than a new pair of trendy pants. Oh well. I choose a mug glazed in a deep blue and head inside to find the mysterious Tink.

A cat (aka allergy bag) brushes past my leg and I try to step aside lest I become hive covered.

"You must be allergic," the bearded guy in baggy overalls says from behind the counter.

"How'd you know?" I ask and immediately see the resemblance between the overall guy—Tink—and Mrs. Dandy-Patinko, my college counselor.

"She only goes to people who can't pat her," Tink explains about the cat.

"Feline unrequited love?" I ask.

He nods and stands up from his position near a pottery wheel. All around him are vases, utensil holders, plates, and butter dishes waiting to be glazed or fired. "You like this?" He points to the slab of clay currently on the wheel. "It's a chip-and-dip sort of thing." It looks more like a piece of strange art, but I give a small nod and smile. "I'm just kidding. It's nothing yet. I just slopped it onto the wheel."

"Oh. I didn't want to offend you. I was . . ." I blush. Two minutes in the pottery place and I manage to make an ass of myself.

"No, you were just being kind. No harm in that." He studies my face as if waiting for something. Then I realize he must know who I am.

"Do you know why I'm here?" I ask and feel like a martian sent to investigate another planet.

"Yes." Tink nods and wipes his clay-covered hands on his thighs and motions for me to come back behind the counter. "But do you?"

I think for a second and unfold the pamphlet. "Not really. It's all slightly surreal."

"Isn't that the way life goes?" His voice is gruff and mellow, like he belongs on one of my albums from the seventies—crooning about smoking pot while admiring nature. "Follow me."

We walk around several pottery wheels, past some drying racks, and out the back door of the barn. Down three small steps, we walk along a path set with giant circles made of pottery and glazed in alternating red and the deep blue of the mug I picked out; Tink leads me to a covered recycling area.

"This is it," he says and pats the side of a huge metal bin.

I wait for him to expound further. He doesn't. "Is there more?"

"Look inside," he says and backs away so I can peer over the edge of the bin.

"Whoa." Heaped inside are pieces of pottery: mounds of red, blue, yellow, apricot, deep purple—triangular shards, random mug handles, and discarded squares. "This is so cool."

"Your aunt knew you'd like it," Tink says.

I turn to face the odd artist and ask, "What did she want me to get here? Is there—I don't know—a big picture that I'm not getting?"

Tink twists his mouth to the side. "You know, I'm not sure. She came here and told me about some sort of puzzle—and being interested in life and the myriad paths it takes, I agreed to give you this . . ."

I wait for him to hand me something. "Give me what?"

"This"—he points to a small barrel of pottery pieces off to the side—"and this." From the chest pocket of his overalls he pulls out a folded note and hands it to me. "Good luck." He starts to head back to the barn. "And that mug you're holding— it's on the house. Enjoy."

"Thanks!" I say and gesture with it, then put it down on the ground so I can read the note.

> Greetings and Salutations (remember *Charlotte's Web*, that book you loved when you were little and how you used to walk around saying greetings and salutations when you were in second grade?)

I grile—grimace and smile—as I remember that. Aunt Mable is—was—in so many ways my memory. She stored up so many days, sayings, and childhood moments that I won't remember now. So it's nice—if slightly embarrassing—to think of saying greetings and salutations like a spider from a novel, but I keep reading . . .

> Remember in *Charlotte's Web*, you got all sad because Charlotte died? All the time you read that book you were worried about Wilbur, the pig, but then—boom— Charlotte was the one to go?

My eyes well up even though Mable's referring to fictional animals from long ago.

> Well, if you're reading this, you know I'm gone, too. But—wait—don't cry yet, Love.

I disobey her and let the tears stream down my face. I miss her.
I can't help it.

> Okay, okay, I know you're crying. And I know your nose
> is red. I'd be crying, too, and then we'd look at each
> other and crack up.

I laugh now because she's right.

> The point of this little puzzle—this web, if you will—is
> to keep you going forward. Too often in my own life I
> felt like I was treading water (or coffee) when I should
> have been making motions. So since I'm not there to
> kick your butt in person, I'm kicking it figuratively. Life
> is all about the pieces, and here's a bunch for you to
> sort through. Once you've looked at them, you'll know
> what to do. Love you to bits—heh.
> Aunt Mable x.

Pocketing the note, I crouch down and begin to look through
the various shards in the small bin. Each one is different—pat-
terned or plain, glazed or gray. First I just look at each one and
put it into a pile, but soon I notice there are three main types:
green the color of the Atlantic in the fall, sort of mossy and
dark with lighter lines on them; a bunch of plain gray ones
with darker lines on them; and ones that are striped blue and
white, like a beach chair. I separate them all into piles just to

make the process less confusing—which of course it still is because I don't know what I'm looking for. I suspect that the process—just following the flow of the pieces and not really knowing why—is part of Mable's plan. She always wanted me to allow things to happen, not to think too much, and in this I can't really think too much, so I just do it.

Then, once I'm almost all the way through the barrel, I notice that each pile contains a mug handle. I take the three broken handles out and look at them. No clue. *What the hell am I supposed to make of all this?*

I head back inside and ask Tink.

"Do these mean anything?" I ask him.

He looks up from the wheel. "My sister says you're bright, that you're headed to a good college."

"I hope so," I say.

"Well, I went to RISD myself. And if I learned anything—which I'm not sure I did—then it was to consider the art not just for its parts but as a whole, and not just for the whole but for its parts."

Oh, um, thanks. You've been really helpful. Not quite. "Oh, okay," I say, and go back outside. For some reason I thought he'd just tell me something, explain the whole thing, but no.

Then, as I'm about to put the handles back down, I notice the dark lines and the light lines kind of line up. So I take each curved handle and line it up. On the outside, the lines are just patterns, but on the inside, the lines and curves form letters.

> Find the matching blue and white mug and drink in all
> life has to offer. Everyone deserves a

The words cut off after *a*—everyone deserves . . . what? I don't know now, but I will if I can find the mug that matches the green one. With my next clue in hand, I take my blue coffee mug from Tink, the note from Aunt Mable, and the mugless handle, and head back to my car. Who has the matching mug? And why?

My cell phone rings, breaking the quiet and my thoughts. "Are you here or what?" Arabella asks.

"I'm on my way—seriously," I answer. "I'm just going to call my dad and tell him I'm alive and well and then I'll get there." So I call home, have the perfunctory but obligatory talk with my dad about being safe and having fun, but not too much fun, and then drive my cluttered car toward Edgartown and the café.

After circling the block for fifteen minutes and dealing with traffic and pedestrians crossing the street with little notice, I double-park outside Slave to the Grind II. Nestled between a bank and a clothing store, but on an angle so it's sort of separate, the café is teeming with people. Good news for business, perhaps bad news for Arabella, whose arms are streaked with espresso, her forehead damp. Doug and Ula, the brother-sister team Mable hired to help run the place, are an example of yin and yang. Where Doug is calm and smiling, Ula is frantic and frowning—hurrying coffees over to the tables, plumping pillows as soon as people stand up from the orange and purple floor cushions, and generally looking miserable.

Not that I expected a marching band to herald my arrival or a chorus of well-wishers hailing me as the latest and greatest ferry transport, but a notice might be nice. Instead, all I get is a smile and cheers from Doug, who looks robotic in his caffeine-charged cash registering, and nary a nod from Ula, who gives off the emotional air of soured milk, until Arabella delivers a frozen mochachino to one customer, wipes up a spill with her trusty cloth, and then sashays over to me.

"Fucking hell, Bukowski, it's about time."

And just like that, summer has officially started.

Chapter 3

A few minutes later, during a lull in the fairly steady stream of tourists and locals looking for an afternoon pickup-up (aka frozen lemonade or ice coffee), Arabella shows me to the narrow, creaky stairs in back of one of the storage closets to our small apartment. Each of the risers on the stairs is painted a different shade of blue.

"Cool—it's like walking up the ocean!" I say as we climb the steps, passing azure, sky blue, turquoise, indigo, navy, and every other blue that exists.

"That's exactly the look I was going for!" Arabella beams at me over her shoulder.

"You did this?" I ask. "Isn't this a summer lease?"

"And your point is . . ."

"Point being you're not supposed to paint or permanently alter the place?" I say and take the last two steps at one time. "I mean, my dad and I don't even move the furniture that much at home—and it's a long-term rental . . ." My voice trails off as I take a second to think about my dad. Right now he's tying up all those end-of-the-academic-year issues, dealing with Aunt Mable's will, and trying to get over his grief by plunging into a trip to Europe with his girlfriend, Louisa. I won't see him until mid-August, when he visits here for Illumination Night in Oak Bluffs, when the whole town is lighted by lanterns. It looks so romantic in photos, but I haven't seen it in person since I was little.

Arabella pauses outside the plain white door to the apartment and waves her hands like a supermodel selling skin cream. "Now—this . . . this is your new home—well, home for a while. But then, everything's temporary, isn't it?"

"Thank you, Lady Philosophy," I say and lean against the wall while she unlocks the door. Once she does, she hands me the key.

"Just so you know, I never lock the door. It just sticks and you have to use the key to unstick it."

"So basically you do lock it," I say and nudge her butt with my knee so she'll finally open the door and let me see inside.

"Ta-da!" Arabella throws her arms open wide and reveals her current masterpiece: our new flat. "The theme is Endless Summer!"

"Like that Beach Boys album?"

Arabella nods and rushes from a wall where she's collaged Hawaiian prints and actually glued retro surfboards to a wicker cave chair suspended from the ceiling by a chain. "I figured we needed to make this place a little glam—a sort of Beach Blanket Bingo retreat from the cappuccino chaos downstairs."

"It's amazing," I say and walk around like it's a dream. Then I think of something. "Do you have any mugs?"

"Sorry?" she asks and points me to a glass cabinet. Inside are rows of mismatching glasses from the sixties—hula girls, surfing guys, a set of shot glasses glued to Matchbox cars. Arabella demonstrates with one glass. "You drink and then race them!"

"But no mugs?" I ask, just in case she's got the missing red mug.

"No, but you can grab one from downstairs." She waits for me to react more to the flat. "Do you like it?"

The small kitchen is part of the main room, but sectioned off with a low wall on top of which Arabella has placed lanterns and lights shaped like stars with diamond-shaped holes cut out—all in shades of blue. "The whole thing just works—forget acting, forget golf putting, you should go into design!"

Arabella hoists herself up onto the kitchen counter and watches me try out the barstools, the striped beach chairs, and the giant inflatable shark, where I sit down, straddling Jaws like the thing's a horse.

"No. Design's just something I like. I'm still game for acting. And the golf—I still haven't been."

"We should go. Not now, but we should drive over and . . . oh, shit." I stand up, tipping Jaws on his side, and then go to the door.

"What?" Arabella hops down from the counter and follows

me, checking her watch. "You're not working until the night shift—six till whenever—whenever being whenever the hell you feel like it because Doug and Ula will be gone by then. Thankfully."

"No," I say, frantically dashing down the stairs. "I've been double-parked this whole time. My car's blocking part of the street—I was just going to run in and . . ."

I get down to street level and find—of course—that my car and all of my belongings, everything—clothes, books, Mable's package, my phone, and my wallet—are gone.

"Oh dear," Arabella says and frowns.

"You curse, like, every two seconds—now my car's been towed with all my earthly possessions in it and all you can come up with is *oh dear*?"

"Oh dear," she says again, this time cracking up.

"It's not funny. What am I supposed to do?" I stand with my hands on my hips. Normally, I'd call my dad or Aunt Mable or just suddenly know what to do, but I don't. "Okay. Get me the phone book. And a phone."

Cut to a half hour later when I've reached the nonemergency police number, been put through to the parking bureau, and told that since it's Saturday past noon, I can't retrieve my car until Monday.

"But I don't have any clean underwear!" I say to the parking person like she cares. "And my phone is in there. And my wallet."

All my complaining gets me nowhere. "I'm going to have to borrow your clothing," I say. "I've been wearing this for two days. And a night. . . ." I pluck my grimy T-shirt away from my skin and then let it go. "I am so gross right now. All I wanted to do was shower and get clean before getting gross again tonight. Now I'll smell like stale beer, BO, and espresso."

Arabella puts on her very English advertising voice. "A new perfume from Love Bukowski." Then she thinks for a second. "You know you're welcome to anything you can find, but I have to say there's not a chance in hell my jeans will fit you."

We stand next to each other and check the height difference for the thousandth time in our friendship. "Yep," I say. "You're still mammoth."

"Mammoth makes me sound fat."

"You're not fat," I say and poke her stomach.

"I know that. It just sounds that way."

"Oh my God. Stop." I sigh. "Fine, you're modelesque—better?" Arabella nods and I go back to my clothing conundrum. "So what do you suggest I do? Go shopping in the two hours I have before serving coffee for the night's eternity?"

Arabella suddenly smiles and winks. "No. Not at all. I don't know why I've only just thought of this."

"What?"

"Henry," Arabella says. "You should phone Henry."

"Because . . ." I stretch the word out like it's a full sentence.

Arabella starts making us a frozen blended drink. "Because his dad owns half of this island. And before you go shaking your head all prim and proper, it would just be a favor."

"I don't know," I say.

Arabella shrugs and glops some chocolate syrup on a mound of shaved ice. "What's the big deal?"

"The deal is . . ." I want to object, to explain that I don't want to be that girl—the one who runs to a guy every time she needs help. I want to be able to build a bookcase, change the oil in my car, and get my car out of the lot after it's been towed. But I also just want my car back and want to get settled without having to wait forty-eight hours. "Give me the phone."

While I wait for Henry to come pick me up, Arabella and I share a giant concoction of our own—shaved ice, chocolate syrup, whipped cream, and a large puddle of mint flavoring.

"The fact that Mr. Randall—sorry, Trip Randall the third—owns the tow lot shouldn't surprise me. And yet . . ." I shake my head. "I'm not sure about these super-funded summer people."

"Hey, you *are* one of those people," Arabella says, and sips the drink.

"No, not really," I say, but maybe she has a point. I don't want to be a prepster and yet I am by sheer nature of my education. I don't want to be seen as having a guy-infested brain and yet by sheer nature of my romantic roving eye—Jacob, Henry, Charlie—I could be. "Besides, summer's the great equalizer, right?"

"Meaning?" Arabella sucks some sugary sludge through a straw.

"Meaning . . . to a certain extent, everyone's got the same

intentions during the summer, so no matter what your financial factor, you want to have fun."

Arabella tilts her head to the side and nudges me. "And just how do you spell fun?"

"Um, f-u-n?" I ask.

"No—try s-u-m-m-e-r f-l-i-n-b."

"Summer flinb?" I ask and crack up. "I'm not sure I'm familiar with that term."

"Oh, shut up. You know I meant fling. Not that you'd be the one to recognize such a term."

"I'm just as much of a . . . flinber as you are," I say like it's a competition.

"Oh yeah? Prove it, Bukowski," Arabella says. Then she lets me sip.

"Listen, it's easy for you. You're . . . modelesque and tan and British and no matter what happens you take off at the end of the summer. I meanwhile . . ." I look at my disheveled self and begin the self-critique. "I look like some Irish girl circa eighteen-hundred-something shoved into the clothing someone forgot at the Laundromat. Not exactly hottie material."

Arabella sighs. "How lame is it that no matter how amazing a woman thinks she is, self-doubt always creeps in?" I sigh back at her and listen. "You are beautiful—quirky, nontraditional—but really pretty. And you know that. You just feel slimy. You slept outside covered in beer and have no Jacob to show for it—which, coming off of a transatlantic breakup with my brother, can't have felt good."

She's so right. Asher and I were a couple. We had that

thing—that fun and hand holding—but it never felt totally good. First, he was off-limits because Arabella objected. When we finally got together officially, I had to leave—and then he pretty much dumped me on my ass after hooking up with someone else.

"All of this doesn't exactly make me want to run out and find another potential heartache," I say and open my mouth to speak more, but she shoves the straw in to shut me up.

"Love, I hereby pronounce you free from your past." She taps me on my shoulder like I'm being knighted. "Look around. Pick a guy you like. You don't have to fall head over heels for him—you just have to *like* him."

"An interesting notion," I say and make a note to consider it.

"It's perfect we're friends," Arabella says and shovels a spoonful of the icy mint chocolate mixture into her mouth. "Who else would eat this with me?"

I shake my head and scoop some up for myself. "No one. That's why we can never break up."

Arabella raises her eyebrows. "Oh, like we're a couple?"

"You know what I mean. Female friendships can be just as great and intense and crazy as relationships. And people do break up."

"Well, we won't," Arabella says. "We're far too mature—or wait—maybe we're far too insane for that."

"Agreed." I lick my spoon, take another mouthful, and then add, "But Mable did."

"Did what?" Arabella asks. Her hair starts to slip from its

loose knot and a bunch of it winds up in our muddy, sweet drink. She licks the ends of her hair and pronounces them delicious.

"Aunt Mable and my—my mother, Galadriel. They used to be best friends. And then they weren't. That's why I asked you about having a mug . . ." I show her the mug handle from Tink's pottery place. "I thought Mable was making a point about valuing female friendship—everyone deserves a . . . What do you think it means?"

Arabella holds the handle and then gives it back. "I haven't got a clue." Then she puts on a heavy *Lord of the Rings* voice. "But I am not the mug bearer."

"Okay, I'll try someone else," I say.

"What makes you so sure it's someone you already know?" she asks.

I *hmmm* out loud and say, "I don't know. I guess it could be anybody."

I look around the Endless Summer flat and smile. The afternoon light slices across the floor, casting blue and gold rays from the window ornaments. Every detail is taken care of. Even the bathroom is wallpapered in old album covers. "Thanks for this, Bels. It really is great."

Arabella smiles shyly and nods, then goes back to sipping until a car horn beeps and she thumbs to the window. "That'll be Henry. He won't bother coming up."

I raise my eyebrows. "Oh, you're intimate with his pickup patterns?"

Arabella ignores my hint and says, "Just get your car and come back in time to work. I did the early shift and I need to nap now. Off you go. And say hi to Henry for me."

I watch her walk to her room, flop down on her bed, and then I walk out the door.

Chapter 4

Outside, drumming his hands on the steering wheel of his antique BMW, Henry mouths along to the Talking Heads' "Once in a Lifetime." I open the passenger door and jump in, putting on my seat belt and giving him a quick hug in one fluid motion and sing a quick *ba-dum-ba-dum* from the chorus, even though it's thoroughly annoying to anyone but yourself when you vocalize an instrumental bit.

"How come you're not singing?" I ask.

Henry pushes his hair out of his eyes with the back of his hand and downshifts into second gear. "My voice is just *that* bad. Trust me, as lame as I look lip-synching, it'd be worse if I tried to do it for real. Not like you. You've got a great voice."

"Thanks," I say. It's a nice compliment but one that's causing me ever-growing worry. For so long I counted on my voice to carry me to adulthood, as if there were no other possibility of what I could do than sing as a profession. But since that certainty is hazy now, the compliment only makes me wish people would notice something else. I remember a girl named Lisa who had naturally near-platinum hair. She had lots of other qualities, too, but Lisa once told me offhandedly that her hair was the only thing people bothered to comment on—not her lacrosse skills, not her *cum laude* grades, not her speech team award (although, come on, who comments on speech team, seriously). So maybe that's what I feel in terms of singing—of course I'm grateful for the kudos, even more grateful I can carry a tune and that singing makes me happy, but there's an increasing awareness that I want more—not more compliments, but more awareness of my other strengths.

"The ride's not long," Henry says, and he gives a small wave before we pull out onto the street. I look back and see Arabella up in the window looking down at us and wonder why she is watching. "Let's go!"

We're off and I breathe in the summer air. Once we're out of the noise and hum of Main Street, we zip along back roads, past farms and houses until we're driving alongside the water. Marshy views and the placid inlets make me feel calm and peaceful—kind of like I usually do with Henry. It's not that he's boring—he's just really steady and sure.

"Thanks so much for getting me, and for taking me"—I look around—"wherever it is we're going."

Henry grins maniacally. "I'm stealing you for my very own . . ." Then, maybe worried his joke revealed something, Henry follows up with, "It's no problem. Really. If I can't exploit my father's power for good, what's the point, right?"

"I guess," I say and grip the rolled-down window as we take a curve half on the road and half on the sandy shoulder. I wonder if I would mind if Henry took me away, whisked me off to his plush digs to wine and dine me. It sounds easy. It sounds fun. It sounds semitempting (um, like there's even been an offer?) but it also would feel distant, like it would be happening to someone else. Like an out-of-body experience.

Henry slows the car down outside a locked chain fence. Everyone has issues with their parents, and sometimes I feel lucky to have the issues I do with my dad—namely that we've been so close he now feels the need to make a point of our independence by making me a Hadley Hall boarder. Aside from that, I don't have many qualms with him. My mother, however—Galadriel—Gala—that maternal mystery is another story. An epic.

"Hey, can you jump out and unlock the gate?" Henry touches my knee to bring me back to earth from whatever parental planet I've been visiting.

"Sure, but I don't have a key." I hold up my hands as proof they're empty and hop out of the car. As I take a minute to look at the lightly worn exterior of the BMW, I remember that Lila Lawrence, my shiny Hadley friend who now goes to Brown, has an old BMW, too. It's like the fact that the car isn't new and glistening makes it less obvious. That the off-beat colors (hers is purple, Henry's is orange) give off an eccentric air rather than just a moneyed one. All those subtleties of wealth—if the cars were this year's model, it would only mean Lila and Henry came from New Money. And New Money isn't nearly as posh as old family money. That much I know.

Henry digs into his glove compartment and finds a key

ring on which are strung numerous brass, silver, gold, and skeleton keys. "It's the big square one with the rubbery thing on it," he explains and turns the music up while I attempt to locate the key. Once I do, I stick it into the giant padlock and wriggle it around until the clasp opens.

"All set!" I yell over the music and swing the gate open while Henry goes through.

The lot is sandy and deserted save for a mess of cars parked in no particular order. "Which one do you want?" he asks and it occurs to me briefly as I watch him wander from Bentley to rusting Jeep Wagoneer to VW Bug that he's only partially kidding. I get the feeling that if I really hoped to leave the lot with a different vehicle, I could merely ask Henry to trade my crappy Saab (my crappy Saab that reminds me of Mable so I will never get rid of it) and he'd make it possible.

"I'm good with what I have," I say and pat the side of my car like it's a dog. Inside, my piles of books and maps and clothes are okay. "Looks like no one took anything."

Henry shrugs and walks over. "No one takes anything here. You know that, right? You can leave your keys in your car all day and night and no one would touch it."

"True. I mean, where are they going to go? You can't get a ferry reservation until October now . . . so I guess you'd be stuck."

He eyes my face, looking for clues of some kind. "I hope you don't feel stuck." Henry peers into my car, probably amazed at the volume of junk inside. "That's a pretty big pack you've got there." He opens the side door.

I thumb to the backpack, "Oh, that's Jim." My face is totally straight. "My pretend boyfriend."

"Hi, Jim," Henry says and offers his hand to my bag. I try not to laugh. "Thanks for taking care of Love on the ride down, but I've got it from here."

He winks at Jim for my benefit and I consider his words. Does he want to take care of me? Am I that in need of rescuing? Granted, Henry was there at Mass General—he saw Aunt Mable as she withered away. He's been pretty sensitive about everything, which heightens his appeal. But then again, we're talking about an improv conversation with my hiking pack.

"Jim's seen me through some good times," I say.

"I bet. He seems quiet but able to hold a lot," Henry says. Then he grins. "I was trying to come up with some metaphor like he's got deep pockets or something, but . . ." It's no surprise that Henry would choose that expression. I get the feeling that despite his relaxed way of being, the fact that his own pockets (or, um, Daddy's) are way deep is a big deal.

I put my hand on the window of the driver's side and check my watch. "Shit. I have to go. My first shift is really soon and I'm about to win the award for least-showered person on the island."

"Runner up, maybe," Henry says and scratches his neck. "But not first place." He scratches again. "Damn, I've got so many mosquito bites already and it's only June."

"Tell me about it," I say and give in to the many itches on my legs.

Henry gives my right calf a look. "Jeez, what have you been doing? Camping?"

Without pausing I answer. "No—more like crashing outside for no good reason . . ." It sounds more daring and cool than it was in reality, but I'm kind of rushing to get out of here and also have the sneaking suspicion that even though I pride myself on not being super-chameleonlike (e.g., I stay myself no matter where I am or who I'm around), Henry and his heavy-hitting money people make me feel like I should be more adventurous than I naturally am. Or maybe that's my psyche telling me I really want to be more adventurous. Whatever. I could make myself nuts thinking about all this.

But Henry raises his eyebrows and does that guy cough-chuckle thing that shows he's half jealous and half shrugging to make it seem like he doesn't care. "Ever heard of bug spray?" He says *bug spray* like he means to say condom—if that's possible. Then he adds, "If you went—camping—with me—I'd make sure to bring some Off! spray—it's the best."

I don't know what he's picturing. Me rolling in the woods with some summer hottie—can you say fat chance? How about me lusting lamely at a high school party? With a sinking feeling, I remember that part of my whole friendship with Henry is built on the pretense that I am closer to his age than I really am. I should just blurt out that I'm still at Hadley—that I'm not a Brown student like Lila. But those are the kinds of corrections that are best made right away. Once you let time go by it's so much harder to tell the truth—like if you don't know someone's name and then you hang out, you feel like an idiot asking later. So I keep my mouth shut.

"I haven't done a lot of camping," I say, wondering if this whole conversation has a double meaning. Haven't gone camping, haven't had sex. Does he know? Or am I wink-nudging myself?

"So sleeping outside doesn't constitute camping?" Henry asks.

I shake my head and open the car door. "It wasn't camping. It was just . . . nothing." Nothing is how I explain my continually confusing interactions with Jacob.

Henry takes a couple of steps backward, his sneakers scratching on the sand. "Usually when people insist something's nothing, it's something."

I smile without showing my teeth and sigh. "You're probably right," I say and drop it. If he wants to think I'm Miss Camping Expert—or whatever we now think camping means—that's his prerogative. "Thanks again for helping me get my car back. I couldn't have waited until Monday."

"It's no problem." Henry gets into his car and closes the door. "Anytime!" He waits for me to drive through the gate so he can lock up and then cups his hand like a megaphone near his mouth. "Come surfing tomorrow. There's a group of us going." I nod and give him the thumbs-up. "Ask Arabella. She knows the details!"

I bet Arabella does know the details. Even though she's my friend and I love her—and I am so appreciative of the apartment and her general presence—it's a little hard for me to totally accept that she's made a name for herself already on the island while I am still new. Of course I've been here for mere hours, but the island doesn't feel like it's mine yet. Maybe after I get settled in at work—if I ground myself in grounds—heh.

Top reasons I know I am not going to commit to a life in the service industry:

1. I cannot get "Would you like sugar in that?" out of my head.
2. Asking people if they prefer one or two percent, full fat or skim is fulfilling only in the sense that it gets them off your back for a millisecond until they insist on seeing just how much froth is on top of their cappuccino.
3. Despite the fact that I'm decent at multitasking (e.g., I can steam milk and plate a side salad with sautéed pumpkin seeds and chevre while answering the phone and repeating for the twelfth time that we're "open until we're not"—the catch phrase Doug and Ula invented that I think is rude but they find cool), the job I have only makes my condition worse.

My condition being SIMH. Sym-huh. Stuck Inside My Head.

"But it's not like you're working in a library," Arabella says when I tell her my career concerns. "And it's not like you're going to be serving coffee for the rest of your life."

"I know, but . . ." I look out at the sidewalk from the window in the kitchen while Arabella slathers on her nightly face mask. "And I'm not trying to be melodramatic . . ."

Arabella mimes violin playing and continues to spread thick algae-colored goop around her cheeks, forehead, and all the way down her chin and neck.

I turn to her and undo my hair from its restaurant restraint (not a hairnet but an old rubber bracelet of Mable's that I sometimes wear on my wrist, other times in my hair). I let the red mass of it fall across my bare arms, covering my face until I'm peering out a hair curtain. "With singing, I get to express myself. And it's just that I'm so caught up in my own thoughts that it occurred to me tonight as I slopped out my millionth latte, that if I don't find a job where I actually do that—express myself—I'll just be one of those mumbling people." Arabella raises her eyebrows underneath the sludge and her face mask shows signs of cracking. "No, I'm serious. You act and get out all of your emotions or you redecorate and have this visual way of getting your ideas across. But what am I supposed to do with my life so that all of this . . . ?" I point to my head like it's a container, which I suppose it is.

"You could teach," Arabella says and watches to see if my ranting and raving is finished for the evening. The red retro clock she hung up near the surfboard mounted as a desk reads just past midnight. I closed the café when a solid fifteen minutes had gone by and no one came in. But did I lock the door? I think so.

"Teaching is a possibility," I say like I'm done with college and ready to go out into the real world. "But I'm not sure."

"Well, lucky for us both that you don't have to decide tonight. Now, I've got four more minutes of being frog woman and then I'm rinsing it off and going to bed."

"Me, too," I say. "Minus the frog stuff."

Arabella peers out the window, looking at the bluish moonlight that casts an eerie glow onto the empty cobblestones. Down the street, bars are open, drinkers and dancers and drunken duuuudes (those prepster party people who end up elongating every vowel) are still only halfway through their Saturday night. Luckily, the café is situated far enough away from the noise that we'll be able to sleep in peace.

Peace until, that is, there's a knocking downstairs. I jump and say, "Ah!" like someone booed me from behind a corner.

"Relax, Bukowski," Arabella says and holds up her finger in the one-minute position while she goes downstairs, her sexy short bathrobe (maroon, silk, quite revealing) balanced only by her clumpy green face. Two minutes later, Arabella emerges from the café and starts picking at her flaking face mask like nothing happened.

"Um, hello?" I stand next to her in the bathroom as she squeezes out a washcloth to finally rid her skin of its botanical beauty regime.

"Oh, someone wanted a late coffee," she says.

I put my hands on my hips. "And did you give this person the last of the stale brew?"

"First off, it's not stale. You just made a fresh pot an hour ago. And second, I just told them to serve themselves."

I'm out the bathroom door by the time she finishes her sentence and I tell her, "It's not a cafeteria, Arabella." What I want to say is that Aunt Mable's café isn't open to the public at all hours. It isn't her place to let post-bar strangers in to help themselves to the leftover croissants and coffee. Arabella's so relaxed in such a debutante way sometimes that she doesn't think about the practicality of the situation.

"It's no big deal," she mumbles from under the wet washcloth.

"Never mind," I say and start down the stairs. "I'll sort it out."

Of course, I was so busy being quasi-critical of Arabella's ease with the café and her lax attitude toward all things normal that I never bothered to ask her who had come a-knockin' for that late night brew, but had I thought about it, I might have come to the conclusion that Chilton Pomroy, aka Chili, would be perkily waiting for me downstairs. But no.

When I take the stairs two at a time, arriving in the café with barely acceptable boxers, T-shirt so worn it's nearly see-through, and no bra I see Charlie and his hippie girlfriend, and I'm awash in fast-reeling thoughts: Why the hell am I in my pajamas; at least my hair is clean and down—I feel prettier when it's down even though I think it looks neater when it's back; glad I met the hippie girlfriend before so she—if not Charlie—doesn't think I parade around like this all the time. And note to self, or rather, note to Arabella: Thanks for not telling me to don a sweatshirt. I cross my arms over my chest and look defiant for no reason, but it's better than baring my breasts for the world.

Admission—despite my desire to appear calm and cool at all times, I am in fact a flustered mess at present.

"Did you get some hippy?" I ask and am horrified by my slipup so I talk really fast to try and cover it. "I mean, coffee? There's lattes and mocha, if I can find the leftover hot choco-late. Or maybe you're more in the mood for frozen lemonade, which is in the freezer—of course—I mean it's frozen, right?"

Charlie, stunning in his navy blue T-shirt—the kind that must feel like silk it's so worn in—and his gorgeous girlfriend (in stable boots, a sleeveless cotton dress that looks like an an-tique slip, and an armful of thin, gold bangles) stare at me like I'm deranged.

And I kind of am. Could I chalk it up (oh, school-year im-agery and it's summer) to the late hour, the lack of sleep of late, the constant whir of the coffee machines, and my ever-slurring thoughts of love, college, loss, and Aunt Mable's treasure map? Sure. But only part of that would be true.

I am a flustered mess because of the guy in front of me.

Charlie does this to me whether I like it or not. Unlike that calm feeling I had with Henry this afternoon, or that con-nected feeling I had with Jacob, around Charlie I feel stereo-typically weak kneed and racy, blushed and beating fast. Thoroughly crushed out—not in a teenage movie kind of way where I notice him one minute and the next I'm distracted by a pair of expensive shoes or the prom committee, but a very real feeling of being crushed by my own emotions.

"You've met Mike," Charlie says as if this serves as a hello. He thumbs to his girlfriend (aka Mike—of course she has a cool boy name). Mike promptly slides over to me and sticks out her hand.

"Not formally," she says and then looks at Charlie and back at me. "That's a fine greeting, Charles."

Her use of his full name startles me—as if I'd never considered that he had any moniker other than Charlie (or Boat Boy). Somehow, it doesn't fit him. Charles is someone in a button-down shirt, reciting Victorian poetry or talking about stocks. Not the guy in front of me with a day's worth of stubble, hair dipping into his eyes, long-sleeved T-shirt streaked with white and green paint, and a body that begs to be hugged.

"Oh, Charles, is it?" I ask him with a grin. If I have to be enamored, I might as well try to get my sense of speech back so I can form somewhat clear sentences.

Charlie rolls his eyes and smirks at Mike. "Okay, Mikayla," he says to her and she smirks back.

Then Mike looks at me. "Daddy favored the Russian writers—thus, Mikayla." I stare at her, probably drooling until she raises her eyebrows and goes on. "As in Vladimir Mayakovsky?" Of course she's one of the girls that refers to her parents in the familiar, like we all call her mother Mummy and her father Daddy. Before prep school I would have heaved, but it's so commonplace at Hadley I hardly notice. (Okay, I notice—but then, I notice everything.)

"Oh, right," I say, like I have any idea what Mike's talking

about. But I note the way she used a Russian accent to pronounce the name. Then I realize I do have some knowledge of
Russian literature (bow now to the Hadley gods) so I say, "Hey,
could have been worse. You could be Gorky or Pushkin."

Charlie gives me a side glance and for a second I allow myself the indulgence that he is impressed that I came up with
two other Russian authors—not that this is a huge feat, but
after my silent shock when I laid eyes on him (alas, only
eyes . . .), this might be a step up.

I think Charlie will explain why he's here at midnight, why
he stumbled into the café—my café (sort of)—just to flaunt his
girlfriend? I mean, he knew this was Aunt Mable's place, since
I showed it to him last year when we met. But rather than explain himself (something he doesn't seem to do all that much)
he says:

"I still remember that amazing moment you appeared before my sight . . . as though a grief and fleeting omen . . ." He
looks out the window as he says this like it's a regular part of
conversation and I can't help but wonder what the hell he's
talking about.

Then Mike touches my shoulder and says, "Pushkin—he's
reciting Pushkin just to show off."

I perk up a little and my heart starts its laps again. Showing
off? For whom? Does he want to inspire a catfight between
Hippie Mike and me? Not going to happen. To prove this I
make myself stop staring at Charlie even though it feels painful
to turn away from him.

"So, Mike, what brings you to my . . . to the café?" I decide

I will befriend Mike. She is friendly, faunlike, and so willowy I kind of want to push her over, but this is only due to the fact that she gets to be with Charlie all the time and I have to get over it.

"I just felt like cocoa," she answers. Mike wanders from the coffee station over to the plush chairs by the front window and sits on the arm of a large leather one and shrugs. "And Charlie likes to give girls what they want."

No, she did not just say that. Now I do want to heave. Except her tone is so blasé; maybe she's just one of those girls who assumes everyone wants to give her what she wants. So why should I be any different?

"Is that so, Charles?" I ask.

Charlie comes up so close he could press himself against me and kiss me, but instead he just reaches behind me for a packet of sugar that he taps on his palm. "It's Charlie. The only people who call me Charles are my parents." Mike laughs at some reference I don't get and Charlie backs away from me and shoots her a look. There's a lot of subtext between them, but even though I consider myself a sleuth of subtext, I just don't get it.

"Well, it's getting late," I say and touch my watch like I'm in a play and need to show the audience just how much past midnight it is. "And I'm on the early shift."

Charlie nods. "Yeah, me, too. I have to get the boat out by dawn."

Mike tosses her hair over her shoulders. "Why bother sleeping—just stay up and do it."

Charlie shakes his head. "It doesn't quite work like that, Mike. Some of us work around here—and boat work is extremely taxing physically. And mentally."

Mike holds up her hand like a stop sign. "Hey, I'm not the one you need to convince."

I raise my hand grade-school style. "I'm confused?"

Charlie finally sighs and shakes his head. "It's nothing. Just a difference of opinion. Mike's of the mind that working is for . . . what did you say?" He looks at her.

"People who aren't creative enough to come up with another option," she says and sips her cocoa.

"She's naive. But then, aren't we all?" He shuffles his feet back and forth on the bare wood floor, then holds his cup of coffee up as if he's about to make a toast to me. "Thanks for indulging me."

"Bye, Love," Mike says as she wafts over to the trash, deposits her cup, and heads to the door. I don't remember telling her my name, but then again it's hard to recall facts and figures as I watch Charlie saunter down the moonlighted street. He has his hands in his pockets, his girl (as in not me) at his side, and I just sit there in the café, indulging myself as I indulged him. Then, if the poetic vision of him weren't enough to send me reeling, Mike sidles up to him and drapes her arm over his shoulder. They're down the street now and I have to rush upstairs and open the bathroom window to lean dangerously far out to see Charlie return the drapage—his arm over her shoulder, her head on his chest.

"Just shoot me now," I say out loud.

Arabella, good friend that she is, appears next to me and sighs. "Ah, unrequited love—bad for the heart but good fodder for the artistic soul."

"I think my soul's just about as artistic as it needs to be," I say and give my teeth a perfunctory brushing before tumbling into bed.

Chapter 5

"So if you look at your color you can find out your shifts for the week," Arabella explains to me over morning coffee with Doug, Ula, and the couple of college students they've hired for the summer to steam, blend, and shout "mocha decaf."

"Am I pink?" one of the college guys asks. "That's cool if I am; I mean I have no problem with pink."

"I'm orange," says the other. "So, Monday morning, then Wednesday night and . . ."

Doug announces, "Arabella, you seem to have everything under control." He smiles his way around the café, and then drags Ula out the door, ever grim and grumpy in her dressed-as-the-evil-character-in-movie black pants and black long-sleeved turtleneck in summer.

"Bye." Arabella and I wave, and I know we're both thinking how glad we are to be rid of them. Doug and Ula leave to catch the ferry back to Woods Hole so they can oversee Slave to the Grind in Boston and Arabella and I give each other a high five.

Back upstairs, I change into shorts and a tank top that used to belong to Arabella's famous-model mother, Monti. "This is so cool," I say and slide it on.

"She wore it for some shoot with the Clash—or the Rolling Stones," Arabella says absentmindedly. "I forget which. But she never liked it—that shade of blue . . ."

I look in the mirror at myself: My red hair is just starting to blond up at the front, the dusting of freckles have continued to conquer my nose and cheeks, and my forever-SPF'd skin is as pale as it is in February.

"You need some sun, girl," Arabella says and flicks my white shoulder.

I turn toward her summer-brown face and sigh. "You might be naturally copper-toned, but I will always dwell in the land of the translucent."

Arabella shakes her head. "Maybe if you got out more . . ."

I sweep my hair into a ponytail and slick some lip balm on. "Yeah, man, I'm a beach babe at heart." I say it like a surfer might, and then I sit on one of the tiki stools and drink my orange juice from a fake coconut. Arabella's sense of design leaves nothing out—even the shower has a grass skirt curtain.

"That brings me to my next point." Arabella shoves the work schedule chart that she developed in front of my face. "See? Everyone has a color. That way you just have to glance at the chart to see when you have a shift."

"I know. I was at the meeting." I nod. "Sounds good."

"And you're blue." Arabella cocks her head and rubs her bare arms. It's still early summer and the mornings are chilly.

Chilly makes me think of Chili Pomroy—note to self: Call her ASAP to check in. "And I gave you less work time."

"Blue—how fitting," I say.

"It's your favorite color, not a mental description."

"I know. It's just . . ." I wonder how to phrase it so I don't hurt her feelings. "It's like you're in charge here and I'm the visiting coffee wench even though . . ."

Arabella completes my thought. "Even though it's kind of your place. I get it."

Arabella checks her watch and pulls me off the stool and down the stairs. "We need to work. Let's keep talking while we grind. Heh."

The morning customers roll in, so I steam milk and plate croissants and cinnamon sticks while Arabella tends to the vats of coffee and hauls a couple of bags of ice from the freezer.

Over the blender noise while I make a frozen chocolate latte, I tell her the rest. "You know in my mind we just served a couple of coffees and hung out on the beach."

Arabella nods and rings up the sales. "That's pretty much what I'd thought, too. But being here . . ." She hands the customer some change and turns to me. "It's actually better than I thought."

"How so?" I wipe my hands on my white apron. Eight in the morning and it's already dirty with grinds, chocolate, and wet from the ice.

"Growing up, I never got to have jobs . . ." She blushes and puts her hands to her cheeks. "This is going to sound so ridicu-

lous. But because Mum and Dad are famous and arty, and . . .
it's not the culture I was born into. You don't just work at an
ice cream shop." Arabella looks out the huge front window to
the swinging sign for Mad Martha's Ice Cream.

"So you're just reveling in the job aspects? Earning money?
Which part?"

"All of it. The responsibility . . . I know you thought I was
off partying before you got here, and maybe I did for a weekend, but I've really taken to having a routine, getting everything organized, and being . . ."

"In charge?" I ask. It's not that I mind. Really, it's more that
I notice that I don't want to be in charge. That I don't want to
work endless hours.

"Yeah. What about you?"

I sigh and pour leftover frozen sludge into a cup and sip it,
giving myself mega brain freeze. "I don't know. I need to work.
I'm saving for college, and I told Mable I would . . . But with
all the stuff that's happened, I just feel like chilling out more.
Like I need to recharge."

Arabella comes and hugs me. "That's what I figured."

I pull away and look at her. "So you're not mad?"

In her ultra-British voice she corrects me. "Dogs get mad,
humans get angry. But no, I'm not." She shows me the coffee
schedule again. "Count how many shifts you have, Blue. Then
look at how many everyone else has."

I study the sheet. "So I'm working less than half time?"

"For now—if that's okay with you?" She says it like a question, so I know it's totally fine if I disagree. But I don't.

"I think pseudo half time sounds about right." I wipe the counters as I talk, and Arabella punches numbers into the cash register. Aunt Mable refused to get computers, preferring instead to buy a giant antique cash register with a jingly bell that sounds every time you make change—jolly enough to make you somewhat forget that you just dropped nearly five bucks on a large cup of coffee.

Arabella unties the strings at the back of my apron and kicks my butt up the stairs toward our apartment. "Go have fun. Go do something. I'm learning business here. You know, valuable life lessons and all that."

I feel guilty, so I whine, "No, *you* should be out at the beach and exploring the island. I should work all the time. You're my guest!"

"I'll tell you when I need a break. Just stick to your serving blocks . . ." She shows me the schedule yet again. "And the rest of the time—go get a life!"

"Oh, thanks, now I feel really cool," I say. But I know she knows me. And I know Aunt Mable—probably even my dad— would agree. My overthinking tends to bog me down.

"Oh, you are," she says. "You just don't know it yet." She gives me a dramatic wink and then rushes back to take orders from the coffee crowds.

Upstairs, I take my time wandering around the apartment, sitting on the surfboard couch and trying on the various garments Arabella has left on coat hooks—not because she wears them, but for added ambience. One shirt is a Hawaiian-print button-down. I slip it on and look in the mirror over the tiki bar; it's a rectangle and oddly placed, so I can see only my body but not my head. But it's enough to let me know that even if my best friend thinks I'm cool, I'm not cool enough to pull off the retro Hawaiian print shirt. I put it back where it belongs— out of my reach.

Chapter 6

One week, two beers, three sarongs, four slurred come-ons from lame-os at the Navigator Lounge, five sun-cream applications (three from self, one from Chili Pomroy, one from Arabella—that is, no one exciting), six slices of pizza, seven jogs, eight frozen lemonades, nine half-shifts of serving coffees and creamy drinks, and—to make up for the lack of decent sleepage—finally ten good hours last night.

I wake up refreshed and famished. Good sleep does that to me: Bad sleep and I can't look at food until a couple hours have passed and coffee has made its way into my system. But good sleep—bring on the bacon. Or bread products. Or eggs. Or—enough. "Bels, I'm heading to the Black Dog."

Arabella's answer is muffled, from the depths of her covers. Despite the heat, she sleeps with a sheet and two blankets. "Bringmebacktwocrullers?"

"If they have any . . ." I tell her and shove some crumpled bills into the pocket of my jeans. It's eight in the morning on Sunday, and if you don't get there early, the best baked goods are gone. "Sleep well," I add to her on my way out the door, and since we've been sort of passing by each other at odd hours of the day and night, it never occurs to me to wonder why she'd want two crullers—and that maybe she's not alone in her bedroom.

After I pay for three giant cinnamon sugar twists (no crullers left), I bag two of them and take the other to the beach. It's low tide and since it's early, the only people out are families with young kids building sandcastles and daring to dip a toe into the cold water. Being island bound is awesome. It's an insular life; we keep seeing the same people over and over again and by now we've eaten in all the restaurants, been to all the beaches except the private ones, and pretty much soaked it all up. But it's great. And being away from emailing, texting, and all the electronic ings is a welcome break. My thumb doesn't ache and my thoughts don't revolve around checking messages every two seconds. Every few days, Arabella and I wander to the local library, where there's Internet access, and check, like we did yesterday:

> Hello, Love!
> If you're reading this, you're probably at the
> library. Glad to know that your island experi-
> ence is still relatively remote. From your phone
> call it sounds like the summer's taking up a nice
> pace. And I think Arabella's onto something
> about not planning and just taking it easy. (Mable
> and I used to confer about your tendency to

overburden yourself.) I know you don't like the
expression take it easy, but I hope you do.
Louisa and I will see you in August for
Illumination Night, if not before—not sure I can
wait that long to see you!
Love, Dad
P.S., I wouldn't feel parental and intrusive
enough without asking about your essays and if
you've started them. I've had the pleasure of
reading a couple from other students and think
it's best if you get an early start as they seem to
require a bit of revision. Xo.

Love that my dad can make me smile and grit my teeth in
one minute. Love that he knows me well enough to tell me to
chill out and love the fact that he's right about the essays but I
hate the fact that he is. The only other exciting email I had was
a mass emailing I found only because I was waiting for Arabella; she took so long to write back to her famous royal ex-
boyfriend, Toby, who still plagues her with long missives about
their old life together. Plus, I saw she had an email from Asher
in her in-box and I was so tempted to read it or ask about it
to see if he mentioned me, but it's a sore subject for both of us
so I didn't. Instead, I sorted through the junk and spam and
found:

Mercury—
For security reasons we have changed the pass-

> word to this year's Malibu gala. The new entry
> code is the fifth planet from the sun. We will
> follow this mailing with a personal call from one
> of our staff.
> Regards, Teeny and Martin

That I received bulk mail from Martin Eisenstein's film company and his wife is just plain funny. But he did say when I met him in England that you never discard an address or contact; you just add them in until you need them later. He can't need me for anything, but he could serve as entrée into the California world of which I know nothing. And maybe it's time I scheme a way to get out there, even if it's only for a couple of days to go to that party, even if it's just for the utterly surreal aspect of going to an event I've seen profiled on television and in celebrity mags for years. Of course, it's an all-blue party (guests are reportedly supposed to be fluid, like water, all the better to mix and mingle) but that's just a drop in the bucket (heh) in terms of problems associated in getting there. I mean, flying three thousand miles is hardly a drop by. But maybe an excuse will pop up.

Notable correspondence missing from email account = Jacob, evil Lindsay Parrish (whom I figured would torment me from time to time this summer with her fall plans for school domination), and anything from my mother. Somehow, with Mable gone and her treasure hunt in full swing, I thought she'd line up a talk-show moment where my mother suddenly enters my life after nearly eighteen years of absence. It's not that

I'm desperate to find her (or obviously I would have made more of an effort), but without Mable, there's a gap. A void where there once was this maternal figure. Of course, I know no one—not even Galadriel (aka birth mother)—could fill the spot Mable did, but my biological and emotional curiosity is piqued. Fifth planet from the sun = Jupiter. That I know this bit of info isn't startling. But the realization that all I'd have to do to get to Martin's party is plan a college interview in California—Stanford? UCLA? Santa Cruz? It doesn't matter which one. Any of them would be cause enough to head out there (or at least validate the trip in my dad's eyes and, um, wallet). Note to self: Head back to the library to check on fares out West ASAP.

Leaving my flip-flops and email thoughts in the car, I walk for a long time, shrugging off the broken mug handle, the search for love and missing mothers, the pre-college perfection behind. Past the gray-shingled houses, past the bloated bluffs, I go all the way until my mind is clear. I sink into the sand and relax in the warmth of it. Even though it feels slightly postcard-Zen tacky, I breathe in and out and wonder what's missing. Then I realize: my journal.

The depository for all my thoughts, lyrics, lists, and gripes, my journal is off on its own adventure overseas. Poppy Massa-Tonclair, my writing adviser in London (and right now on the *New York Times* bestseller list as well as the recipient for that famous literature prize) has it. She let me know she received it but hasn't given me a grade or comment. Then again, it's kind of an unusual final project—and while I hope she knows it's not a cop-out, part of me is very aware of how revealing it is. The unedited me is not something I show that frequently.

The journal thoughts lead to thoughts of college, of applications and essays I have yet to write, which leads to my as-of-yet unrouted college tour, which leads to heart palpitations and very definitely not the summer Zen I was seeking. So before stress sucks the sun from my day, I look at the waves. Who told me to count them? Oh, yeah—I remember Charlie holding me by the waist and telling me to count the waves to calm down. It works—as long as I don't think of him.

If I had my journal, I'd make a list of things to do. But maybe that's the point. I shouldn't make so many lists. I should just do what I want. So I dig my feet into the sand and don't realize I've fallen into a light napping state until I sense I'm being watched.

"Hey," Henry says and touches my thigh with his bare foot.

"What'd you find?" This from Jay Daventree, one of Henry's college friends.

"A girl!" Henry shouts and smiles. "She washed ashore and appears to be human."

"I'm part mermaid," I say and sit up.

Jay and Lissa and a bunch of Henry's friends who look vaguely familiar wave as they create a beach oasis with chairs and umbrellas and a portable grill.

"Fancy seeing you here," Henry says and sits next to me.

"I should say that to you . . . This is a public beach, right?"

Henry looks at the water and slides his shades from the top of his head to his eyes. "Yup. Jay decided he wanted to mingle with the masses."

"How charitable," I say and smirk.

Henry shrugs. "Basically, I think he worked his way through the girls at the beach club and needs to cast a broader net."

I laugh and stick out my tongue. Say what you want about Henry and his money and his crowd, but at least he's aware. He doesn't live in the financial oblivion that so many of the posh people do. "Maybe I should stick to swimming at the pond this week," I say and pretend to fend Jay off.

Henry takes off his shirt and I sneak a side glance at the abs on display. "I'm heading in. Care to join me?"

I point to my tank top. "I don't have a suit."

Henry raises his eyebrows and grins. "This girl here says she doesn't have a suit!"

As if this is a bat signal in the sky, Jay, Jason Landry, and some other guy run over from their beachside antics and, with Henry, carry me on their shoulders and swing me like a kid into the waves.

"Ah! It's freezing!" I scream and sound so girly I want to puke. So then I brace myself for the cold water.

"One! Two!" they shout. Jay has my ankles and Jason has my arms.

"Fine—I can take it!" I say and close my eyes as they fling

me into the air. But I never land all the way in the water. Instead, I land in Henry's arms. He holds me there in laundry basket carrying position.

"Sure you don't want to go for a dip?" he asks.

I consider it, then feel myself shiver. "Well, I'm already kind of soaked." I look at him—he's so tempted to throw me in. "Oh, go ahead, you win. You can . . ." But before I even complete the sentence Henry swings me at full force up into the air and when I land this time, I am in full bodily contact with the chilly Atlantic Ocean, not the safety and warmth of his arms.

I pop up through the water, my skin tingling from the salt and from the experience. Right now, I am that beach girl. That tank-top clad woman who gets hoisted from the sand by hottie guys and chucked into the water while squealing. And maybe it looks dumb from a distance, but in the moment, it actually feels pretty good.

"How about a back rub?" Henry asks when I'm all dried off and wrapped in his oversized blue-and-white-striped beach towel. The pattern makes me think of something but I can't remember what.

"Sure," I say and spread out the striped towel, lying flat on it. Henry starts rubbing my shoulders. Arabella and I made the definitive list of back rubbing techniques and situations, feeling that all back rubs can be analyzed for content and goals and Henry's mastery of the art is no exception:

1. The "you look tense" back rub—one person rubs the other person's shoulders so they can "relax."

2. The pre-hookup back rub—you both know where this is leading, but you go through the pretense of it anyway to either delay the, um, gratification or so one of you can pretend to be naive.

3. The "I give the best back rubs ever" game—you declare this so that the hottie guy has to accept and you get to check out his stunning shoulders. In the reverse, the claim is made by the other person and you're all "Really? I don't believe you. Show me" And then it goes to rule #2 or to the next rule.

4. The "can't tell if you're interested in me or not" rub. More tentative, this back rub involves lots of conversation (compared to say, #2, which can be totally silent) to gloss over the fact that the two of you are touching . . . a lot.

5. "Seriously, we're just friends." Aka, if I could be totally honest I would admit I have feelings for you. But I can't bare my soul, so I'll just grin and bear it.

6. JBR—the jealousy back rub is the massage equivalent of slow dancing with someone hot for the sole reason of making your ex (or crush) jealous. Involving intense moans to up the ante helps (e.g., "Oh, __, that feels great—you have such strong arms!").

7. The "my parents gave me a gift certificate at a spa and the masseuse taught me this great back rub technique. Can I try it out on you?" Of course, you use the opportunity to try to perfect it (e.g., "Wait—let me try to remember. Is it clockwise and then counterclockwise or counter-

clockwise and then clockwise?" and such "lapses of memory," all of which just give you more excuses for letting your hands roam around). Big plus: you can improvise, moving down to the upper thigh. "How does it feel here?"

8. The "I'm sitting behind you in the team van bus, your shoulders are right there . . . so, why not just start giving you a rub?"

9. Make up an Asian-sounding back rub technique and claim that you learned it on a summer exchange program. "When we were on the night train traveling from Jinzhou to Bei-zhu, we were bartering with the train conductor in our carriage. In exchange for two cartons of Marlboro Reds, he taught me the ancient technique known as Chi-tse-zhang-bo-ku" (upon the utterance of the technique name, you close your eyes and make a reverential bow). Then, you take total control of the situation, saying—as you lead the person to a bed or something—"Here. Now you try it."

10. The disclaimer: "I kind of suck at this, but a bad back rub is better than no back rub, right?" The answer: Unlike a chocolate-chip cookie, which is always better than not having one, a back rub that sucks just plain sucks. And if you get one that is really lame, you can't help but wonder—is this person kind of lame? The guy who struts across campus but is all drippy when it comes to back rubs, well, that's telling you that he's just got a facade. And the girl who seems all sultry but rather than

massaging you just digs her nails into your skin and kind of presses? She's not as sensual as she seems.

So while getting a good back rub rocks, a bad one is enough to dissuade me from a crush—maybe. Henry kneads his way down my back, stopping just shy of my ass, and then retreats to the safety of my shoulders. So he's a game player. At least, that's what Arabella would decide upon seeing this. But then again, maybe she's gotten a Henry Handling herself.

I turn my face away from Henry so I can see the ocean and go back to thinking about back rubs. Arabella and I discussed, decoded, and deciphered all the techniques—you've got your strong but gentle; your playful; your finger-poking; your touchy-feely hemp-clad, sandal-wearing, Grateful-Dead-String-Cheese-Incident-listening flat-palmed rub; and then— the most common, most egregious back rub bonanza—the subtle side into front rub. While this is a great prelude to rule #2, when you're just friends with someone, having them try to sneak a feel is not allowed.

And it's this common front rub that I'm expecting Henry to try, but instead he is stuck at a solid rule #4, jabbering away—either out of nerves or lack of anyone else to talk to, since his friends are either surfing or asleep on their elaborate beach chairs.

"How's that?" Henry asks while his thumbs sink into my back.

"Good," I say but blush. It's too sexual—too revealing. Well, it's not really, but it feels that way because I'm in a tank top, which, when you consider the area covered, is really like underwear, and there's no way in hell I'd lie in my bra and underwear and ask Henry to rub me. So. So I'm about to object when he turns the tables, sliding from rule #4 into rule #3.

"I hear you give killer massages," Henry says like massage is something involving nudity and oil.

"Oh yeah?" It comes out flirty, but really I just want to know from whom he garnered this info.

"Lila Lawrence told someone or something—I don't know. It came up at a party this winter while you were abroad."

"While I was in London people were discussing my back rub prowess? Gee, I feel famous."

Henry stops rubbing my back and I sit up, pulling the striped beach towel around me both to fend off the wind and to cover up my rather revealed-feeling self.

"It was a passing comment," Henry says. "Just one of those party things."

"Where was this party, anyway? I feel like I missed out." I say it so he knows I'm joking, but he answers me.

"Lila's beach house in Newport."

"Ah, the off-season extravaganza." I remember visiting Lila's house (house = one of the old Newport mansions circa *Great Gatsby* with a gilded ballroom and an indoor pool complete with heated floors lest the wealthy feet get a tad cold). She's big into off-season parties because her mother is all about the in-season parties. "Must've been fun."

Henry smirks, remembering something. "It was."

I raise one eyebrow at him so he knows I'm watching his face, looking for signs of lascivious thoughts. "No, not like that." Henry laughs and commands me to rub his shoulders, which I do, and find myself intrigued by his physique (I mean, he plays college soccer and rows—read: hot body) and annoyed that I'm so shallow as to be swayed by a guy's shoulders. "A bunch of us proved a point . . ." His voice trails off.

"What happened exactly?" I ask and rub his arms, working down to his hands, which are warm and smooth. When I start to massage his palm, he squeezes my hand, which makes me nervous.

"It's kind of a long story—one for another time. But the text message version is that this guy we're friends with—or used to be friends with—was working at . . ." He looks at me. "Let's just say we taught a friend a lesson and the party went on from there."

I shake my head. "Sounds complicated." Henry looks at me. Then he keeps looking at me. With that look that can mean only one thing. He's about to lean in and . . . "Oh my God!" I say it way too loudly, especially considering Henry's about five inches from my face.

"I'm sorry," Henry says and backs away, embarrassed.

"No, no," I say, trying to reassure him that I wasn't shoving off his attempt at a kiss (though I'm not sure if maybe my psyche was speaking for me).

"I thought you . . ."

"No—it wasn't that," I say and touch his shoulder so he doesn't think I'm totally blowing him off. "I just remembered something." I point to the striped beach towel. "This is the same exact pattern as . . ." He'll think I'm nuts if I talk about the mug handles at Tink's, but I do it anyway. "Henry . . . do you have a cup?"

Cue the *you're crazy* look. "What?"

"A mug—a coffee cup. Do you have one you're supposed to give me?"

Henry pulls me to my feet. The swim, the salty massage, the breeze, the interrupted kiss—all in the past as he walks me to my car and I explain the mug handle situation.

"So you're trying to find your missing piece?" he asks, with the emphasis on *piece* as in *ass*.

"Not that kind of piece," I say. "But glad to know your puerile humor can transcend any conversation."

"I wish I did have a mug handle for you. It's kind of a cool thing . . ." Henry helps me inside the car and then closes the driver's side door. I lean out, for once enjoying the fact that because the car is black it has absorbed the sun and warms my freezing arms.

"It is a cool thing, but it's frustrating not being able to find out what the next clue is . . ."

"Don't you think that was part of her point? Like, just live and enjoy it and see when it appears in front of you?" Henry looks at me, maybe thinking about the almost-kiss, and his words are meaningful. He's correct and compassionate and there's no real reason not to kiss him, but that small moment has passed.

"Thanks for the swim," I say. "I have to deliver some doughnuts to Arabella." I point to the white paper bag on the seat next to me.

Henry gives that reverse guy nod, tipping his head back, like he's trying to flip a light switch with his chin. "I'm having a dinner party—would you like to come?"

"A dinner party? How civil. Are you sure it's not a bonfire or catered drunken barbeque?"

Henry laughs and waves to some stunning girl on the beach. Then I realize the stunning girl is Hippie Chick, aka Mike, Charlie's girlfriend. I want badly to ask how he knows her. But maybe he doesn't. Maybe he's just one of those guys who waves to hot girls in suits. "I decided this summer needs a little glamour."

"Sounds fun. When is it?"

"Summer solstice."

I nod. "The shortest night."

Henry takes a couple of steps backwards as I put the key in and start the car. "I figured with all that daylight, people'd want to use the night hours wisely . . . to . . ." He pauses and shrugs. "To whatever."

"Sounds like a good toast." I cheer him with my Nalgene water bottle. (It's a yellow one, which I bought only because it was on sale and then once I filled it I realized it will always look as though it contains pee. Note to self: Next time splurge on the color that doesn't resemble bodily fluids.) "To whatever!"

Henry's up on the dune, right near where Mike is lying down (I can spot her raspberry halter top and her sun hat on the sand), and yells down to me, "Love!"

"Now what?" I smile and yell back. He really is so cute standing there in his bathing suit and tan.

"The Midnight Hour!" he shouts like that makes any sense beyond being a song that, while good, is way overplayed by every high school band that thinks they're the next white-boy blues-influenced group. Then, because he knows his words didn't make sense, he adds, "The dress code—it's 'in the midnight hour.' Interpret that as you will!"

I don't ask him who else will be there. I figure it'll be the usual group, the same sunny faces from the beach and café, but who knows. I drive away, with the windows down, the warm air breezing in, wondering what kind of dress that really means—basically, it sounds like a full-on excuse to wear lingerie. If I had to guess, I'd expect Jay Daventree and Henry to wear a Hugh Hefner getup, and maybe Jason Landry (whom I believe Arabella has already "back rubbed") will don some cheesy boxers.

I envision a bevy of beauties wearing nothing but baby doll nighties, garters (like that's such a common thing to wear at midnight), bustiers, and silk robes sans undergarments. Not for me. I don't see Halloween as a reason to dress as a slut—if I want to wear a catsuit I'll do it when I want—and I don't want to be the breast-centerpiece at a party (with rather sizeable breasts; a little cleavage tends to go a long way on me). So no matter what the suggested dress code is, I decide I'll bypass the French maid's uniform, the bra and panties set as dinner wear, and do for something else. What exactly that is, I have no idea. But I know someone who will.

Chapter 7

Correction: two someones.

"Arabella!" I shout as I come up the stairs to the flat and nudge the sticky door open with my knee. "Rise and shine. And start thinking about what I can wear to a dinner party. I'll trust your advice."

"What about mine?" comes a voice—a male voice—from her room.

With some trepidation I slide my feet along the floor and pause outside her doorway, averting my eyes in case some random guy is in there and I have to choose between saying something lame like "have fun last night?" or a quiet lecture about the risks of the random hookup.

But of course the face in front of me is not random, yet it's certainly a surprise.

"Well if it isn't the lovable Love!"

"You know I hate that," I say and do a dramatic run, leap, and hug to Chris, who responds with an equally ardent embrace. "What are you doing here? Why didn't you call? And how come you slept in here and didn't tell me you'd arrived?"

Chris gives a *heh* as a laugh and responds, "Sit down, share the baked goods you brought back, and all will be explained."

Arabella whisks off to the café to check on the state of things and to get us all mud slides while Chris and I lounge in the surfer's nook—the small area off to the side of the living room that's covered in plush faux-lambskin and decorated with tiny glowing surfboards even during the day. If I meditated, I could do it in here. But since I don't, it's more of a reading space or—once I get a new one—a journal-writing place.

"So it's off with Alistair?" I ask and make a sad face to Chris. "I thought he was your first big love."

"Me, too," Chris says. "But maybe we just put too much into it. It's one thing to have an intense couple of days of being together on vacation . . . but it's something else when you try to move that sort of idealist romp into reality."

I nod and tuck my knees to my chest. "Yeah, I bet that's what would have happened with me and Asher, if he'd ever managed to make an appearance."

Chris taps me on the knee. "Um, we're talking about me? Focus."

"Right. Sorry for the brief self-sidetracking . . . You were explaining."

Chris lies down, looking like he could make a snow angel in the plush white wool rug. "I got to California and it was awesome—just what I expected. We hung out, made out, dined out. But after a couple of days it felt like . . ." He sighs. "Like it was fine."

"Fine?"

"Fine."

"You don't like fine," I say.

"Nope—and neither do you. Fine is boring. Fine's like, I could be doing other things—other, better things. Fine's sort of why bother, you know?"

"So you didn't stay there?" I ask.

"I probably would have, to be honest. I mean, Alistair's smart and funny and gorgeous and likes me. I seriously doubt I'm going to do better—even if it only felt fine. Or okay. But then I got a phone call . . ."

"This is all very dramatic," I say. "I wish Arabella would hurry up with our slides so I'd have entertainment snacks while you spill."

Just as I say this, Arabella comes back in, managing to carry three oversized plastic cups filled with mud slide chocolate and red straws. I rescue her from imminent spillage and the three of us fake surf in the living room while Chris goes on.

"Apologies to Arabella for the repetition," Chris says.

Arabella flings her hair back from her shoulders and shrugs. "It's fine by me. I'm not sure what kind of recall I have after last night." Only when she says this do I notice the row of empty Matchbox car shot glasses lined up by the sink. Apparently I missed a late-night session last night.

"Hadley called me. Of course they called my parents first. But more on that later. They want me to start a GSA. You know, a gay-straight alliance? Which I'm kind of psyched to do." I open my mouth to say something, but Chris doesn't allow me. "And no, not just because it's good for college apps. I also like the idea of leaving a legacy there. Like I came out to relative support—if you subtract the few guys in the dorms who ignore me . . ."

"What about your parents?" I ask. "I know you told me they called my dad for periodic check-ins."

"Yeah, not my mom so much, but my dad—anyway, they're sort of past that but still don't want a giant reminder of 'my choices.' " Chris makes air quotes and puts on a funny voice. "And the GSA is an honor, but it's also a fairly big banner—a gay banner—so that's something I'll have to deal with this year."

Arabella holds her head, trying to massage last night's alcohol and her current brain freeze away. "But now you're here."

"Right," Chris says and begins to clean up the kitchen. "Assuming it's okay with you, Love, I'd like to crash here for a while."

"Of course," I say. "But what ever happened with Alistair?"

"Oh, he's off at some ashram in Asia now. Very earthy-crunchy, white slacks and a gauzy shirt. Not for me." Chris washes the Matchbox cars and grins to himself.

"Wait a minute. I know why you're here," I say and poke him in the back. "You have an agenda!"

"Don't we all?" he asks and holds up his soapy hands.

"What's going on?" Arabella asks. "Intrigue?"

"Chris is here for a visit—true. But I'll bet he plans on visiting someone else while he's on the island . . ." I wait for Chris to say something, but he goes back to cleaning. "Chris's crush—Haverford Pomroy."

"Oh, right, the could be straight, could be gay . . ."

"And Chili's bother. And of course they live in Oak Bluffs, a full ten minutes down the road."

Arabella whacks Chris's head with a dishcloth. "And here I was feeling flattered that you chose to visit me . . ." Then she heads toward her bedroom. "By the way, Love, what'd you do this morning? We were waiting for hours for you to come back from the Black Dog."

I swallow and turn so she can't see me blush. For some reason I feel weird about telling her I was with Henry—even though I wasn't with him, with him. "I was at the beach," I say and leave it at that.

"Did I miss anything?" Arabella asks. "Anything exciting?"

"No," I say and throw out my empty mud slide cup and close the bathroom door so I can shower. "Nothing at all."

Chapter 8

My favorite shift at the café so far is the morning—crack of dawn to noon. Then I've made some tips (bless the tourists), worked enough to feel slightly virtuous, and still have the rest of the day to explore, swim, or just walk around town, which is what I'm about to do with Chris, Chili Pomroy, and her brother, Haverford, on whom Chris's crush has only gotten worse since arriving. I figure going out with friends will get my mind off Charlie. We had a one-sided run-in this morning—one-sided meaning I saw him and he didn't see me (am I really that unnoticeable?) down by the public docks. He was tying up a small rowboat. It's a common sight in the morning. The yachties get their crew to row in to get them breakfast or the more ablebodied among them do it themselves, feeling very proud and muscular in their khaki cut-offs and faded yacht club T-shirts. Poor me—I was so tongue-tied and lusting from afar that I went right out and bought a journal at the stationery store. Just one of those speckled green and white class notebooks that always look like a relic from the 1950s or something. Currently, mine is empty save for one line: *I can't stop thinking about Charlie.*

My dad called this morning to say hi and asked me if I'd "met anyone"—like this was a normal convo to have with him. I told him I hadn't because it's too complicated. I didn't want him saying something like if Henry doesn't see what's in front of him . . . or if Charlie doesn't trade Hippie for me . . . or any parental pontifications. So I kept mute and told him only that I made up my mind about visiting schools in August—after my time here is done. I can't be doing shifts one minute, then ferrying and driving to all the schools I want to see. So college will have to wait until the end of the summer.

All morning long I've steamed, served, sloshed, restacked lids, rung up sales while I ponder my crush status. Why do I long from afar? With Charlie, it's partially because I got burned before. He left me waiting for him (aka stood me up) before, and he'd probably do it again. That, plus he's got himself a girl-friend. And something about Hippie Mike tells me she's not a summer fling, that she's here for the long haul. She's way too comfortable—I've seen her with the fishermen at the docks, with the preppies at the Newes Pub, and barefoot on the beach, looking poetic and impossibly pretty in a way I proba-bly never will. Boo hoo for me.

So an outing with friends will get my mind off my Char-lie thoughts and off my unrealistic expectations for tonight's fancy dinner party with Henry. Not that I'm going *with* Henry. Just that he'll be there also.

Chris comes into the café with Arabella, and she and I go through the motions of switching stations—that is, she takes over where I left off. She just got up, I've been up for hours, and now I'm off for the day and she's on until late. Every once in a while she closes early, but Doug and Ula are back in town as of this evening, so she's determined to look mega-professional. I, meanwhile, am content to shove off after I clock out.

"Grind well," I say to her.

"Right back at you," she says and makes her own coffee before attending to the oversized filters that got delivered a few minutes ago. She places one on her head. "Do I look hot or what?"

"Ever the actress," I say. "You look good in everything you eat." She takes this as her cue to hang a croissant from her ear, which makes me crack up. Chris tugs on my sleeve. "Okay, okay—we'll see you in a bit."

Outside, Chris and I drive the now-familiar route into Oak Bluffs. "I love this song!" he says and turns up the radio. We've been listening exclusively to WMVY, the Vineyard radio station.

"Me, too!" I say.

"Yet another thing we have in common," he says when we've slowed to a stop at the intersection.

"Oh yeah? What's the first?" I ask. Chris nudges me to look to the left, where Charlie's red pickup truck is idling. Out the passenger window is a length of hippie hair, lolling in the sunlight.

"We both like people we can't have," Chris says and before I can get wistful he adds, "Yet."

"Yet," I repeat, like saying it will make a difference, and then I keep driving.

"I'm in the mood for Mexican," Chili says when we meet her in Oak Bluffs.

"Let's ride the carousel first," Chris says and points to Flying Horses, the oldest working merry-go-round in the country.

"I'll pass," Haverford says. He doesn't roll his eyes as if to suggest Chris is even more gay than he announces himself, but it's clear that Haverford in no way intends to park his ass on one of the painted ponies—even in teenage irony.

"I could go for cotton candy," I say. The reality is that I've been wanting to go to Flying Horses but not in that drunk-slash-silly way when you and your friends are essentially long-ing for childhood but making fun of it at the same time. I want to go on as if in a romantic movie scene, when the lights are all twinkling and Date Guy and I are the only ones there—or maybe it just feels like we're alone because our chemistry is so amazing. Never let it be said that my fantasy life isn't active. Some people have computer porn, I have movie romance. They're both kind of addictive.

"You and your sugar jones," Chris chides and surveys the scene. "Actually, I'm over this place—let's go somewhere else." I can tell he isn't over it exactly, but wants to go along with whatever his crush says—an understandable but wishy-washy thing.

Chili slides a red elastic from her wrist and attempts to

wrangle her corkscrew curls into some semblance of order. Her skin is dark and her eyes are light, the same watery teal as the choppy surf nearby. "How about the farmer's market?"

Haverford nods. "Good deal. Let's take Jaws."

"Jaws?" Chris and I overlap with each other and follow Haverford and Chili on foot back to their parents' cottage. Unlike the misnomered cottages of Henry and his friends, Chili's cottage is a real one—in the gingerbread style of the town, it's painted purple, green, and white, with detailed moldings and a small porch, where Chili and I wait while Haverford and Chris go inside.

"What exactly is Jaws?" I ask. "Aside from a classic movie."

"You'll see. It's no big deal, but Haverford's into it. Figures." Chili shakes her head at her absent brother, making me wonder if she knows the scoop behind his orientation. There are many signs that point toward gay and many others that point toward prepster ambiguity slash straight—and it's still anyone's game.

Haverford comes out (of the door, not the closet, sadly for Chris's sake) and announces, "We're good to go." He dangles a set of keys looped with a circle of twine and we follow him to a shed. Tucked behind other tightly crammed colored cottages, the shed has no lock and when opened reveals a bright yellow squat dune buggy with an open top and no doors.

"Hop in," Haverford commands and we do, with Chili riding shotgun.

Under his breath Chris says to me, "The car's got to be a sign of *huh-ness*." Chris and I say *huh-ness* every once in a while when shouting gayness doesn't seem to be the best move. It's also code for cool and trendy—like Chris will hold up a pair of pants at Rage, the store in town, and say, "Check it out—these are so *huh*." Gotta love the jargon.

I'm about to answer when Chili says, "Isn't Jaws awesome? It's from the actual movie—my dad worked on it and my mom was an extra or something and they somehow got to keep this car."

Haverford smiles and turns left, spinning the cartoonish wheel with his knee. "They like it because it can only go thirty miles an hour."

Chris looks at Haverford in the rearview mirror. "It's very cool."

"So what's our plan, exactly?" I ask. Leave it to me to take wandering as something with an end goal.

"We're just hanging, Love," Chili says and puts her feet on the dash.

"In some cultures, the word chill is used to describe this act," Chris says.

"I get it, okay?" I ask and pull my hair into a bunch so it stops whipping my face as we wind past the ocean and head up island toward the farmers' market. Of course, I don't mention that part of the reason I'm feeling slightly uptight is my pre–dinner party nerves. I'm not nervous per se, more that combo of excited and kind of weirded out by the thought of seeing all the beach boys and bikini girls all fancified. And the fact that it's not at Henry's house makes it even more of an event—of course it started out as a small, intimate dinner party, but as of the message Henry left on my voice mail yesterday, the dinner is now being held at the Manor Club (aka "my family comes from money, but we never mention it"). I'm not really a Manor Club kind of girl—and yet I want to go. I want to get dressed up and see who's there and what might happen. So I figure I'm venturing there part as an observer—an onlooker of the high life, if not exactly a true participant—and also as a single woman. Despite the eye candy on this island, I've yet to do more than drool (figuratively, of course, I'm not that desperate). And Arabella and Chris are convinced that I will come home from the dinner party as part of a couple—if, that is, I come home tonight at all. Henry did mention that it's a summer solstice party and therefore apt to last well into morning.

The farmer's market is in the front yard of the old school, with stalls and carts assembled to display the wealth of colorful fruits and vegetables, home-baked pies and breads, honeys and cheeses. As soon as we're there, amidst the throngs of vegetable buyers, I scan the crowd for Charlie. It's a habit I've noticed only lately—that I look for him not so much because I think anything will happen, but because he makes me feel . . . feel what? I don't know—off-kilter and racy and pensive and . . . But he's not here. When I do spot him—even from afar—I basically swoon. Old-fashioned, dreamy, swoon. Except that I don't get him—that prize goes to Hippie Mike.

"Louisa would love this," I say, thinking of my dad's girlfriend. "She makes cheese at her place in Vermont."

"You like her," Chris says in a half question half statement.

"I do. No one's going to be perfect. I mean, it annoys me that she rearranges the spices in the cabinet and that she got rid of my dad's ancient sweaters, but what can you do?" I wander over to the pies and ogle the variety: blueberry, apple, strawberry-rhubarb. Mable considered pie to be its own food group and suitable for any meal. "With my aunt gone, and with college . . . I guess I don't want my dad to be alone. Do you know what I mean?"

Chris nods and picks up zucchini bread. "I'm buying this. But yeah, I do know. Also, I was thinking about your mother—Gala—and thinking that it's probably good if your dad has someone now."

I know what he's getting at and nod. "Like if he were single and then I met my mom—it could get all *Parent Trap* and that would be so dumb."

"Exactly. Plus, it's kind of like seeing someone who broke up with you. You want to be in a position of power."

Chris is nothing if not psychologically aware, and of course he's right about all this. When I picture meeting Gala—an event that doesn't seem really distant anymore—I want to be in a good place, not needy. And I guess I want the same for my dad. I don't want him to seem like he's still crushed, seventeen years later.

"Try this." Haverford comes over and offers me and Chris a bite of his purchase.

"I'm sure we'd both love to bite your cookie," I say to Haverford because I know it'll make Chris crack up, which he does and has to pretend to examine the pints of blueberries to avoid being totally obvious.

After the farmer's market, Chili, Chris, Haverford, and I drive Jaws the dune buggy to the Gay Head Lighthouse (yes, the real name, though Chris and I called it the Huh-Head Lighthouse for the whole ride) without so much as a trace of irony from Haverford. We take our picnic to the lighthouse lawn, where the wind is particularly active.

"So basically you're looking for someone with a mug handle for the next clue?" Chili asks.

"Yup—why, do you have it?" I shout to her from up the hill, where I peer into a viewfinder to look across the sea.

"No, but would I tell you if I did?" she asks.

I walk back toward her. "I don't know. I didn't think of that."

"What if whoever has it is supposed to wait for a certain time, and then spring it on you . . ."

"You might be right. I have no idea. I can't think about it too much or it drives me crazy and I start wanting to ask everyone I pass on the street if they are the missing piece."

Chili climbs up a big rock and sits there, her tight curls hardly moving in the fierce wind.

"I feel like a heroine in a romance novel," I say when I stand on top of a big boulder that faces the steep cliff that overhangs the shore. Chili joins me and we cling together for balance. I'm so glad she'll be at school next year, even if she will be a lowly sophomore and I'll be a senior.

"Me, too," Chili says. "If they actually had short, biracial girls on the cover of those books. You know what?"

"What?" I shout as my hair flies back in the breeze and my face feels like it's being vacuumed off.

"I'm gonna write one—and have it be about this girl who's half black and half Jewish who finds love on the high seas or something."

"Speaking of high seas . . ." I say and notice Haverford slinking off to smoke something behind a shed.

Chili shakes her head. "He's got romantic trouble. That's the only time I've ever seen him indulge."

I leap off the rock and pull Chili down so we can walk toward the dune buggy. "What kind of problems?" I can't help but do a little investigating on Chris's behalf.

Chili bites her top lip. "Um, I can't really go into it . . . but Have's kind of caught between two worlds."

Chris catches up to us on our walk back to the car and nudges me to try for more information.

"Kind of to Have or Have not?" I ask. "Sorry—I couldn't resist."

Chili laughs. "Lame but funny. Anyway. Yeah, it's like that song my mom always used to sing—*Did you ever have to make up your mind?*" She sings the last part and I join in. *"Pick up on one and leave the other behind . . ."*

"Hey," I say, "you have a good voice!" I don't mention that the song she sang is by The Lovin' Spoonful and how I put it on a mix for Jacob at the end of this year—just because it had a utensil in the band's name—and only realized the blatant lyrics afterwards. Note to self: Check the songs and lyrics twice before committing them to a CD.

"Thanks," Chili says, blushing only a tiny bit. "We sound good together." Once we're in the car, she hands me the keys and we wait for Haverford.

I ask, "Are you going to do more singing at Hadley this year?"

Chili twists her mouth. "I might try out for the Hadley Hummers, even though that's got to be the dumbest-ass name ever."

"Yeah, it's pretty much the ridicule of all the extra-curric groups. Members usually go by the Hadleys . . . But the singing's good . . ."

"What about you?" Chili asks me. "Any thoughts about the future of your illustrious career?"

Cue big sigh and shrug from me. "Not sure."

Chris leans forward. "Yeah, Love, what's up with you and the voice? You were all over anything music related and now . . ."

"And now I'm just not sure, okay?" I snap at him, and he reels like I pushed him. "Sorry. It's just a confusing subject for me. I used to be so sure about wanting to do that, planning my life around it, and this past year it just kind of changed. Or shifted."

"Hey, guys." Haverford saunters back and slides in next to Chris in the backseat.

"Next time you're heading to the smoky mountains, you can catch your own ride back," Chili says to her brother.

Haverford shrugs and stares vacantly out toward the water. "Let's go, Love. I have to take my half-baked brother home."

"Want some company?" Chris asks Chili. She nods. And in the rearview mirror I think—I can't confirm, but I think—that I see Haverford smile.

"I wish you could come with me," I say yet again.

"Believe me, so do I." Arabella gathers the receipts from this morning's cafe take and puts them in the office. "But if Doug and Ula get here and find the place virtually unstaffed, we're in big shit."

"I know. I know." Then I feel bad and guilty. "I should stay with you. Seriously."

Arabella slips a fresh half apron on and sits down for a sandwich. When you work the late morning to the afternoon, there's not really time for lunch, so I usually eat a tuna sandwich at ten a.m. and then by the time I'm done, lunch isn't until four or so. She shoves the soy butter and jam into her mouth and talks at the same time, sounding like she's got a mouthful of cotton balls.

"You know I don't mind, and if I did I'd tell you, right? Isn't our friendship based on honesty?"

"Yeah," I say and look away.

"What?" she prods. "What's that look for?"

"Nothing." I turn away again.

"Oh my God, it's like acting for the stage for people who suck at acting . . ."

"Fine," I say. "If you're going to interpret every single one of my actions then I'll tell you. But I feel funny about it—and I'm worried you'll be angry . . ."

"Enough of the disclaimers," Arabella says and glugs some milk, clearing her mouth so her voice goes back to normal. "Just tell me. I probably already know, anyway."

"Why? What do you think I'm going to say?" I ask and understand suddenly why my dad gets confused when he hears me talking to my friends. He says it's like we're discussing air with a passion—nothing, but something.

"I think it has to do with something—or someone—you want, but something you perceive as off-limits."

"Well, you're right about that." I sit next to her and eat her leftover crusts, my favorite part of sandwiches. It's those little details about me that I think make me seem more alterna than I really am—or like I'm trying to be different. Not that I want to be a total chameleon, but I also don't need to stand out to feel special—I just like crusts.

"Spill it," Arabella commands. She stands behind me and twists my hair up into various silly up-dos that I would never feel comfortable wearing. "You should wear it like this tonight . . . you know, mix it up a little." She holds my hair in a complicated twist with the requisite amount of messiness so that it doesn't look too done.

With her walking behind me to keep the hair in place, we go to the bathroom so I can check out the style for myself. "Very elegant," I say.

"But not too prom, more like 'pouty model on the way back from a wedding' cool."

"I like it," I say and then, when we're both looking at my reflection in the mirror, I add, "It's about Henry."

She looks shocked. "Really?"

I spin and face her. "Why? What'd you think I was going to say?"

She shakes me off. "Nothing."

"No, tell me," I say and feel that wash of sweat when you know you're about to argue with your best friend.

"I thought you'd want to know about Asher . . . but that, you know, you felt a bit guarded asking because of everything that went down in London."

"Oh," I say and wonder if it means I'm totally over him because that's not what I wanted to ask at all. Okay, maybe a little. "Asher's in the past."

"But Henry's in the future?" Arabella asks and waits for me to go on.

I shrug but in the *let's not fight* way not in the *whatever* way. "It's not that I like him. It's more that I feel like there's some weird vibe with him and you and me."

Arabella drops my hair and sits on the closed lid of the toilet. We stay there in the quiet, semi-blue light of the bathroom and I sit on the edge of the tub. "Love . . ." Arabella picks at her cuticles, then looks at me. "First off, I want to say that tonight's your night to go have fun. Drink, eat, and be merry, and hang out or hook up with whomever you like."

"I love that you said whomever."

"You can take the girl out of Britain . . ." Arabella starts, but then her smile fades. "Have you and Henry gotten together already? Is that what you're trying to say?"

"No," I say and shake my head. "Not at all. I mean, he gave me a back rub on the beach . . ."

"So basically he wants to . . ." Arabella looks sad, but determined not to show it. I can always tell how she feels—not because of her eyes, like everyone always says, but because of her lips. Her mouth gives everything away, the way the corners tug down just slightly.

I shrug and shake again. "I can't really tell. But how do you feel about it, Bels? You look—"

"If he liked you . . . or if he tried to have you sleep at his place tonight, would you?"

"Would I sleep with him? No. No way. But the idea of kissing him . . ." I picture Henry's grin, his friendly face, his beach body. "He does give a girl ideas . . ."

"I think you should do what you want," Arabella says all in one breath, and it's as though I can hear her uncompleted thought "as long as it's not with Henry."

My friend and I stare at each other and then I slide backward into the bathtub and land on my butt. She pulls me out. "So there's nothing else you want to tell me?" I ask. She shakes her head. "Then why did it—does it—feel bizarre to bring his name up?"

"I don't know. Maybe it's too triangular or, like, if we have to tell each other every detail of our time with him it just feels competitive."

"Maybe that's what he wants," I suggest and slick Arabella's deep blue-red lipstick on my mouth, blow an exaggerated kiss to myself, then wipe the goop off with a tissue.

Arabella smiles from one side of her mouth, a look that always makes her seem like she's tasted something sweet. "Nothing's bizarre as long as we tell each other. The not telling you was the weird thing . . . And the not hearing from you. When you came back from the beach that day and Chris was here, I kept waiting for you to sit me down and tell me the story like you do—you know, first he said this and then you said this and he looked at you like this. And now I know he gave you a back rub. But nothing else, right?"

"No—nothing. But, see, why are you so curious?"

She sighs. "I think since Toby cheated on me I see every nondisclosure as a betrayal or something. It's like knowing all the details, being in the loop, makes me feel more in control."

"Do you miss him?" I ask. I don't add the *even though he treated you like crap and cheated on you and is overly infatuated with himself.*

"I'm so over Tobias." Arabella pulls me out of the bathroom and into her room so she can change into her "Doug and Ula are coming" work outfit (less summer sloppy and more black pants and a standard white T-shirt). "And with Henry . . . just have fun—or don't. But tell me all about tonight, promise?"

"I promise," I say. "I will narrate fully and even act out entire dialogues."

"Good."

After a minute of quiet I hold up a dress for potential

wearing, then put it back in the closet—too plain. Then another one—too little black dress, not enough interest. "If you liked someone, though, would you tell them?"

Arabella asks, "Why, considering doing that yourself?"

I shrug, even though I am considering that—always considering that, actually. I could tell Charlie my lingering feelings despite his couple status with Hippie Beautiful Mike or I could just march up to Henry and tell him he'd be a first on my list of casual hookups, or even call Jacob, profess my feelings, and see what happens, but it's all too dramatic for me, all too attention seeking. Or scary.

"You mean if I had the kind of crushes you do? On whom?"

"I don't know—on anyone. What if you liked . . ." I can't think of anyone whose name doesn't carry weight.

"Fine—say I liked Henry? Would I blab about how I feel?" Arabella squints. "Never!" She stands up on her bed so she can check out her whole body and outfit in the mirror. It's the only way to approximate a full-length mirror in the apartment. "Whoever the guy is, if he wants me, he knows where to find me. Otherwise, forget it. I chased Toby all over the place. I'm not about to make that same mistake again."

"Fair enough," I say. And I'm glad for her. I am. The thought does occur to me that maybe she does actually like Henry but won't admit it—even to me. And the reality is that she and Henry make much more sense together than he and I would. He's much more in the game and center of attention than I usually go for, and he's got that money issue lurking in the background. Not that I'm convinced I'll wind up with someone who is penniless, but somehow it feels like we'd click better, have a better understanding of the real world. Or maybe that I wouldn't have to blend into his world, or he into mine; we'd just sort of meet in the middle.

"Promise me I can do you hair before you leave?" Arabella asks when she's near the door.

"Yes, fairy godmother. I'll stop by the café on my way out." I curtsy for no reason.

"You'll be the belle of the ball," she says, and then she leaves me alone so I can pick some music to put on, so I can get ready for the dinner party, so I can admit to myself that I am actually hoping for some kind of romantic evening—not a lot, just a little. Is that so much to ask?

Chapter 9

The entrance to the Manor Club is marked by two enormous white statues. Curved and smoothed to polished perfection, they are meant to look like two curved hands welcoming you inside the property. Welcoming you in, that is, if your personal worth is upward of one hundred million and your family name is known in the business sections of the *New York Times* or financial papers worldwide. Staring at the white comma-shaped behemoths now, I think that they are far from resembling hands (even though, yes, art is open to interpretation): instead they resemble fangs.

Set back from the ocean with lawns enough to play football (though that would be most unacceptable), the Manor Club is host to many an island wedding and gala event. That Henry is having a dinner party here shouldn't surprise me, but it does. Money seems to bite me in the back when I'm least expecting it, or when I nod off—like with the Hadley students who hang out at lunch and eat the same crappy deli meats as I do but then when spring break rolls around they're not holed up watching reruns like I am; they're off jet-setting to Istanbul or Ibiza. Even Arabella every once in a while seems plucked from another (more profitable) planet.

The wind swirls my thin dress around my legs and I pull my gauzy wrap close to my shoulders as I walk in between the white fang statues toward the main entrance. I note that there's no gate, no security check-in—not because it's an open club. No, even more exclusionary is the no-gate scene: The place is so exclusive, they know no one would dare try to enter without explicit permission. That permission comes in the form of either a family membership given at birth (not kidding; Arabella pocketed one of the guidebooks for members—heh—and we took turns doing dramatic readings from it) or an invite done by hand in calligraphy that is all very French circa eighteen-whatever.

My personal invite I have tucked in my bra mainly because I have no bag with me and in the mule heels I foolishly chose to don this evening, I'm afraid I'll drop it and be denied entry to what will probably be the dinner party of the summer.

The wide driveway is blanketed in crushed shells that glow in the moonlight. The whole main building is symmetrical—the driveway is a large arch shape, and the main manor house is plucked into the middle, with eight illuminated antique streetlights on either side. At light six I stop and rummage in my breast area for the ticket. Of course, the small slip of paper has slid almost under the left one like it's seeking shelter from the breeze, so I have to dig around for it. Nothing like standing in front of an old money club touching your own chest—

and nothing like doing so and then realizing you're being noticed by someone.

"You okay there?"

I blush hard, but in the night at least it's not super obvious. "I'm fine, Henry, thanks."

"Well, if you need help . . . just let me know." He's a shameless flirt, especially after the beachrub—somehow, the post–back rub familiarity has led to a lot of speculation about underlying tensions.

I remove the ticket and my hands from my bra and display only the ticket for Henry. "See? I've got my Golden Ticket."

"Ah, shame you retrieved it without another pair of hands," he says and offers his arm to me. I take it and the two of us crunch our way up the driveway to the long marble staircase that leads up to the main building.

Outside the enormous doorway, Henry pauses and turns to me with a serious, less-flirty voice. "I'm really glad you came tonight, Love."

"Me, too," I say and wonder what the night has in store.

The first thing the night has in store is my reaction to seeing the theme of In the Midnight Hour come to life. Beyond the slinky dresses (from many a young lady, read: I wore the contents of my underwear drawer because I could) are flowing fountains of champagne, tables set with individual pocket watches as the place card holders, personal menus, flowers, and several giant clocks all set to midnight.

"It's very Gatsby meets Dalí," I say and realize how pre-

tentious I sound, but I can't think of any other way to describe it.

"Isn't it great?" Henry's friend Lissa agrees. "It's even better
than his birthday last year."

I hesitate to ask what that involved and focus instead on the
scene to my left, right, and center. Henry's wearing a smoking
jacket from the 1930s and tuxedo pants, and while some of his
friends take his cue and dress in elegant silk pajamas, or a dinner jacket and bowtie, there are a bunch of people who have
interpreted the midnight hour to mean the midnight hour in
a music video. One girl, in a leopard thong and matching
bustier, is shuttled over to the club office, where she's given the
option of wearing a cape "to cover her buttocks" (I overheard)
or leaving.

"Screw the cape," the girl says. "I work hard for this ass."

I stifle a giggle and do what I normally do in crowded, un-
familiar settings where I am on the outskirts of the social hem:
I go to the bathroom.

Of course the ladies' powder room is an event unto itself,
with various shades of cream and lemon to complement the
Calcutta marble sinks, and the plush sitting area complete with
a vast array of toiletries and makeup. And the flushing mecha-
nisms in the oversized stalls are operated by a discreet button
you press with your shoe, lest your hands be required to do
anything improper, like flush.

By the room-length mirror, I check out the outfit I chose
from Arabella's stash of Monti castoffs. Having a mother who's
a model has its benefits, even if most of the clothes are floor

length on me. My dress is one part flapper, one part nightie. In a much-muted plum color, it's fitted through the top and ribs with gold straps just thick enough to hide evidence that I need to wear a bra. The bottom of the dress is slightly flowy, and lined with a thin underskirt in lighter plum that makes it look like it could be nightwear, which I guess tonight it is.

My hair is in Arabella's tangly twist—very windswept despite the complete lack of wind. Two giggling girls come in—one in a black camisole and silk boy shorts combo, the other in an outfit that could only be called slutty angel, and I stare for a minute before heading back out for some nibbles.

"Champagne?" Henry offers me a tall flute filled with the bubbly and I sip at it while we stand at the edge of the dance floor. The club turns a blind eye to any underage drinking; besides, most everyone is in college already. "Check out Jay and his women."

"He's got a way with the ladies, I guess," I say and watch blond Jay as he manages to slow dance with two nightgowned women. "I guess they don't mind sharing."

Henry puts his arm casually around my shoulder, not close enough so that it's a come-on, more a buddy stance with underlying tension. I like the weight of his arm, the way he smells like some cologne that would be advertised by showing something outdoors . . . maybe a sailing competition. "Would you?" he asks.

"Would I what?"

"Would you share someone?" Henry pulls me a little closer. I can feel the velvet of his smoking jacket and maybe I'd be more attuned to the fabric and the boy underneath it if weren't for the ultimate vision in front of me—gorgeous beyond belief. If it were the credits of a film he would be "Hot Guy in Suit at Party," but since it's not a movie, I have to stare until it's bordering on rude, until I realize it's not some random guy that's making me drool, but Charlie.

"You know him?" Henry asks, watching me watch Charlie.

"A little," I say and avoid looking at Henry so as not to give away my feelings. Plus, Charlie—in a suit!—is dancing with the ever-effervescent Hippie Mike, who looks not so much like a mellow hipster tonight but more like a French ingenue, with full lips and tousled bedroom hair and the requisite slim-fitting, body-hugging slip dress in pale, oceany blue—no bra (read: nice headlights). I cross my arms over my chest and then remember Mable once told me that particular stance made me look defensive—and that Asher said the same thing. Is that what we do in life, remember the things people have told us and then alter our mannerisms or words or actions accordingly?

"Charles—what a guy," Henry says sarcastically.

"Charlie?" I say nonchalantly. "What's his story?"

Henry waves to a girl in a pink baby doll dress and she blows him a kiss. "He's got you calling him Charlie? That's cute—that's nice." Henry clears his throat and laughs in disgust. "Charles is here only because of Mike—"

"She's pretty incredible looking," I say because it's the truth and I refuse to be one of those women who cuts down other women around guys just in the name of self-promotion.

Henry nods. "Oh, she's hotter than hell—but . . ."

"But?" I elbow him, and he tightens his grip on me.

"But, well, she's kind of off-limits, right?" He watches Mike dance with Charlie—they're doing some version of swing or something that involves lots of dips and laughs. The music stops and Henry taps his champagne glass to signal silence, which ensues rapidly.

"Please find your places at the tables—and thanks for coming to a timeless event—this is the shortest night of the year and hopefully one of the best . . ."

As Henry speaks, I watch the faces of his friends, his father—Trip Randall, island real estate magnate—as he downs one glass of champagne and reaches for another. Everyone looks happy, summery, wealthy. Then I look at Charlie—Charlie who drives a pickup truck and makes a living as a fisherman—and feel terrible for him (even though he ditched me at dinner last year). To be out of your element feels pretty sucky. Then I notice Mike staring at me and I look away. When I look back, she's got her arm around Charlie's shoulder and whispers something in his ear. Charlie's response is to look directly at me and for a full minute all we do is lock eyes. With each second that passes, I expect him to look away, or expect that I'll back down. But as Henry speaks and someone gives a toast, all I do is look right back at him. There is no denying it. There's a connection there no matter what, no matter that his stunning girlfriend is next to him, that we're both slightly out of place at the Manor Club, nor that Henry's arm snakes around me again right as Charlie decides to walk over and offer a greeting.

"Love, it's always a pleasure," Charlie says, sounding overly formal. Probably he feels he needs to be formal in this setting—and who wouldn't—except it makes him seem even more out of place.

"Charles Addison." Henry stretches out the words as if the name alone is enough of a hello and stretches his arm all the way around my shoulder, pulling me snugly against him.

Charles Addison. I guess I forgot his last name—Arabella and Chris and I just called him Charlie Boat Boy for so long. Or maybe I never knew it. But Addison sounds familiar. Note to self: Google search pronto. Further note to self: Stop being so prep school and assuming that everyone—or everyone's names—means something or connects to something.

Suddenly Henry pulls me tighter and kisses me on the cheek (Charlie stares at this, but doesn't react in the slightest—to my dismay. Not that I thought he'd leap on a tabletop and scream in protest, but maybe a flinch?) and then announces, "Well, it's time to eat, so we should take our seats. Love, you're at table one a.m."

He leads me away and I look for my name at table one a.m. but don't find it. Amidst the clock centerpiece, the trailing vines of flowers and gold-rimmed plates, there's no trace of a pocket watch place card with my name.

"I swear I know you're supposed to be here," Henry says.

"I have my doubts," I say as a joke, but inside I'm thinking maybe it's a sign—that I'm not supposed to be here and I belong out with the masses, working at the café, hanging out with regular, non-roman numeraled (i.e., Henry Randall IV)

people. Or maybe I will forever be in denial about my own ladder-climbing. "But here's Mike's name."

Right as I say it Mike traipses over, sipping her alcohol and smiling at me, all lazy and pretty, and slides into her chair without Charlie anywhere. "Charles is outside taking a break," Mike informs me and then turns her attentions to Henry.

Henry, caught between wanting to find my place and the new attention from Mike, puts one hand on my shoulder, the other on Mike's head, since she's already sitting down. "Love, you were sitting right here—but someone must have rearranged the names . . ."

Mike looks up at us and grins, drunk but still functioning. "Never mind the seating chart; how about another round?"

I stand there awkwardly wondering where to place myself given the fact that the neighboring tables are full and the only people now standing are me, Henry, and the serving staff. Maybe I should just take a tray and start dishing out salads and cocktails. "I'm just going to run to the bathroom," I say as the lamest excuse possible—how pathetic to make another trip to the powder room as an avoidance tactic.

"When you get back I'll have this all sorted out," Henry assures me, but Mike's hand on his thigh tells me otherwise. I look around for Charlie, wondering if he'd be thrilled to see Mike's hand straying, but then I remember he's outside.

And in a momentary lapse in judgment (chalk it up to the champagne and lack of seat), I bypass the bathroom, carrying my drink, my shawl, and my pride (which I thankfully didn't leave back in the dining room with all the occupied seats) to the back of the manor to the large terrace that overlooks a wide expanse of lawn. The night sky is dotted with stars, the ocean is right ahead of me, and so what if I don't get any food or a place setting and Henry's too distracted by Charlie's girlfriend—the view's nice.

"No seats available?"

I turn so my back is against the cold stone of the carved terrace railing. "No," I say to Charlie. My breath is held in my throat, my skin immediately chilled as he's close enough to me that I can feel the warmth emanating from his body. With one hand on the stone railing, Charlie reaches inside his jacket and pulls out a slip of paper and turns it slowly, revealing to me my own name.

"Behold your place card," he says and hands it to me with a flourish.

Annoyed, I furrow my brow and snip, "Why'd you take it? Just to humiliate me?" I should have known, really. Anyone who stands you up can't magically turn out to be okay, even if they are incredible eye candy.

Charlie's face changes from sly to concerned. "No—no—I didn't mean that at all . . ."

"Sure, just like you didn't mean to stand me up. Thanks. I appreciate the kick in the butt, really." I say it all, glad to have gotten my line in after all this time, and I pivot on my borrowed heels and listen to the *click click* of them on the stone.

Charlie grabs my shoulder, causing me to turn around so we're face-to-face. "I never stood you up . . ."

My mouth drops open, incredulous. "Oh my God—how

can you say that? You invited me to dinner after we . . ." I don't want to relive the kissing, the family talks, the fireside cuddling with him—it's all too revealing now. "You asked me to dinner and never showed up. I think that's pretty much the definition of standing someone up. In the dictionary of my life if you go to *stood up,* it says *see night with Charlie on Vineyard.*"

Charlie looks like he could laugh or get pissed. "In theory I stood you up—"

I don't let him finish. "In theory? A theory is conjecture—the opposite of fact, actually—so you're wrong. You did, in fact, not show up. You didn't only think about not showing up; you did it."

Charlie laughs—it's so tense and we're both so adamant, that it helps break the moment a little, but it's still every bit as intense. "If you'd let me speak, which you seem to be unable to allow, you'd find . . ."

"Fine, speak."

"Fine—let me." Charlie gathers his thoughts for a moment, and I stand with my hands on my hips, aware of how cold I am, how much annoyed I am with him, and how much I want him to just grab me and kiss me, forgetting all the reasons why I shouldn't want this.

"Come inside, though. It's cold," he says and of course, I go with him.

Chapter 10

Inside, Charlie motions for me to follow him down a corridor, down three short steps, and into a parlor room furnished with oversized leather club chairs, a fireplace the size of a soccer goal, Oriental rugs, brass lamps, and a chandelier that Charlie immediately dims by touching a switch on the wall.

"You know your way around here," I say and try not to picture him dating the Manor Club girls who fly in for weekends, host teas, and then take off for the Hamptons or Nantucket, Newport or Europe.

Charlie gives a quick answer. "My grandfather served here. I used to come with him sometimes."

Now I picture a grandpa version of Charlie—basically him with wrinkles and white hair—and imagine little boy Charlie and his grandfather serving drinks from big trays, dealing with all the rich society requests for extra olives or onions, cherries for the Manhattans. No wonder Charlie seems both at home here and resentful of the lavish surroundings.

"So," I say as I perch on the edge of one of the brown leather chairs across from Charlie. "Defend yourself."

"I'm sorry you see it as a defense . . ." He stands up and faces the fire, the embers glowing neon red and orange. "You're right, Love. I shouldn't have left you sitting there. And it does seem like I stood you up. The only reason in my mind that my actions didn't qualify as standing you up was because I didn't want to."

I shiver, both from the chill easing off my skin and from his words—is he a bullshit artist or for real?

"So you're saying that because you didn't want to stand me up, it didn't count?" I ask, my voice quiet because the room is librarylike, demanding soft tones. My stomach growls and I remember I have yet to have any dinner, despite the fact that I'm attending a dinner party.

Charlie takes a couple of steps closer, so the front of his legs brush the front of mine. He pulls me up and the sheer feel of his hands on mine is enough to make me want to pass out. But by some miracle, I don't. I just stare at his face, his mouth, the way he bites on his lower lip, trying to explain his thoughts. He backs up and sits down on the cushioned green bench that surrounds the fireplace. "I had every intention of being there that night. Only a total asshole would have missed that opportunity."

I don't bother to tell him that I've called him that in my head for nearly a year, that I haven't been able to think of him without that night slapping any good memories in the face. "But you did . . ." I sound sad, sadder than I should for just a brush-off, but I liked him, and who knows how different my year might have been if he'd shown up.

"Mike was ill," he says suddenly. "She . . . how to put this tactfully? She swallowed a few too many Tylenols and . . ."

"Oh," I say and now I feel like a jerk. "You were with Mike." Then I realize—he was *WITH MIKE*. While he was kissing me? "So you cheated on her, stood me up, and then rescued her? How gallant."

"What? Cheated on her?" A huge smile comes across his face and he starts to laugh, but I'm still flustered and annoyed. "Mike? You think I'm with Mike?"

"Oh—she's just a FWB? Either way . . ."

"Mike's my sister," Charlie says. "She goes to Exeter and was pretty depressed her senior fall—last year—and . . ."

In truth, it's so much info that I don't know what to consider first: that Mike is not Charlie's girlfriend, that he rushed to her aid rather than desert me for no reason, or that she goes to Exeter when I thought she was this island local who mixed with the summer crowd.

"So Mike just graduated from Exeter?" I ask. "Is that how she knows Henry and these guys?" I gesture with my arm like Henry and his buddies are in the room with us when really they're dancing and drinking and enjoying the shortest night—all without me.

"We all grew up together," Charlie says. "Though you wouldn't know it . . ."

I shake my head. "You mean you knew Henry during the summers?"

Charlie sighs. "It's complicated." I imagine he doesn't want to get into the typical townie versus preppy discussion, and I don't want to wound his pride or anything by making him seem somehow in competition with Henry's heritage.

My stomach makes a last-ditch shot at being placated with food. The growl echoes in the high-ceilinged room. I put my hand over my belly. "Oops. I never did get dinner."

Charlie heads over to the doorway, standing by the bronze plaque on the wall. Each room, each corridor at the Manor House seems to have a plaque named for some fancy person who, Arabella and I read in the handbook, had been a founding member of the club (read: so wealthy, WASPy, and white that they are immortalized by the plaques). "Come on." Charlie beckons. "Let's get you some food and I can explain . . ."

With each step I take toward him, I'm aware of all the distance I've tried to put between us—the hurt at being stood up, his off-limits status as a taken man, his disinterest in me—and how none of these appear to be real. He holds out his hand to me to pull me up the step and as he guides me to food and explanations, I happen to look at the bronze plaque: *The Addison Room.* Charlie. Charles Addison. Charlie.

"When you say your grandfather served here," I ask with my hand in his, "I take it he wasn't serving appetizers?"

Over his shoulder, Charlie looks at me and grins, his eyes sexy as hell, his lips taunting me to kiss them. "Serving—on the board of trustees . . ." he says and like that, his boat boy image starts to fade—and I follow him away from the bustle of the Midnight Hour dinner party and into the Vineyard night.

Chapter 11

So much for the midnight hour—try the early-morning hours complete with stars, sand, and so much sexual tension I can hardly breathe. But as of yet—no kiss. Not even a peck from Charles Addison. Charles Addison who is not as previously assumed by me to be a penniless local fisherman but the American equivalent of financial royalty—a family whose name is a corporation.

"So the Addison Building at Harvard?" I ask. We're sitting on the small stretch of beach near Charlie's cottage, our bare feet burrowing into the wet sand.

"Ours."

"And the Addison Building in New York right near where I interned at *Music* magazine?"

"Ours."

"Huh." It's all I can come up with—I'm just too amazed at my own superficial assumptions and the reversal of them.

"I wanted to tell you—well, no."

With my arms linked around my knees, I swivel so I'm facing him rather than the ocean. Back at the Manor, Henry was busy romancing every hot woman in a slip dress (read: tons) and didn't notice when we slinked past. "Start from the beginning—and go slowly. Apparently I'm in need of remedial social inferences instruction."

"Okay . . ." Charlie stands up, his dinner suit pants rolled at the ankles; he points a tanned toe into the sand and draws a line. "Here's where we met. Or when I saw you."

"On the street—with Aunt Mable when she called out to you."

Charlie shakes his head. "No. Before then."

A smile lurks on my mouth. He saw me before then? Or noticed me? I like that. "Go on," I say.

"I was on the ferry early in the morning that day and I saw you board. I wanted to talk to you, but then you kind of disappeared and when I figured out where you were, you were sharing a dessert with Henry Randall."

I think back to that day. "It was a sticky bun."

Charlie looks disappointed, like the fact that I remember what I ate with Henry means I love him or something. "It was a really good pastry. And I love sweets."

Charlie grins. "Fine. So that brings us to here." He draws a mark in the sand with his toe, continuing. "So I didn't talk to you then. But I—I wanted to. And then there was the street incident, which made me smile all day."

"My aunt had a way of embarrassing me in public—but in a good way." I stand up, too, and place my feet on the line Charlie's drawing in the sand. Every time he talks, he pushes the line forward and I follow on it.

"So then I rescued you and your dad . . ."

I cough in mock disagreement. "It wasn't exactly a rescue. I mean, we would have gotten out of there eventually." I want to add how gorgeous I had thought he was then and how badly I'd wished he'd want to talk more, but I don't. I have no idea where all this is leading.

"And then your dad tried to give me money."

I shake my head and put my arms out for balance like the sandy line is a tightwire. "He meant it to be nice—and you didn't take it—and you were on a boat. So I just kind of thought . . ."

"You did what we all do—assume someone's actions or their surroundings explain who they are. But . . ." Charlie keeps extending the sand line along the beach and I keep walking on it, stopping when he does. "And part of me liked that you thought I was just this person. This island guy with no buildings, no memberships, no real estate."

"I do . . ." I start, and then cover it by adding, "How come you didn't tell me your—oh my God, I almost said your real identity. Like you're a superhero or something."

Charlie runs his hand through his hair and then shoves his hands into his pockets. In the clean white moonlight, the beach nearly glows and his eyes are bright when he looks at me. "What was I supposed to do? Walk up to you and announce my status? The thing is, it's not mine. It's my parents'. And that's what I was trying to tell you that night at your cottage . . . in front of the fire."

In the movie version of this, he'd remember kissing me

then and run over to me and do the same now, but it's not a movie, it's late, and we're cold and on a beach, and he just stays where he is. "Did you know that I thought you were this local, hard-working guy?"

Charlie shrugs and scratches the stubble on his neck. "I was a local hard-working guy. That's the thing. Just because I come from money doesn't mean it defines me. And I don't know— maybe I had some idea that you'd misconstrued something, but it was all pretty hazy in my mind."

"In what way?"

Charlie makes a big loop in the sand and reaches down for a driftwood stick to use as a pointer. "See here?" He points to an invisible spot on the sandy chart. "This is when I was sixteen and an asshole and thought my trust fund would make me a worthy, cool person. And here, this is before that—when I was young and naive and thought money made no difference. We summered here, but I'd play with the local kids or hang out with the farm workers and be genuinely surprised that there wasn't a future in our friendship."

"And what's this?" I use my toe to point to another destination on the line.

"That's when I tripped and fell in the mud in Harvard Square and my pants fell down—it has nothing to do with what we're talking about."

I laugh and point to another place. "Okay, fine. Here."

"So then I got to college and it all kind of got crazy . . . the Euro crowd versus the old money blending in with the regular kids, the public school or Midwestern ideal—it all got to me. Like who the hell am I in all this?"

"Wait. Back up. I don't even know where you go to school."

Charlie gives me a look—that look that tells me I do know. "Oh," I say and clue in. "Oh! You go to Harvard?"

"Thus bumping into me at Bartley's . . ."

"What a shitty day that was," I say. Asher broke up with me on the phone, Mable got worse, and I felt like hell by the end of it.

"Thanks—it was good to see you, too."

"I didn't mean that," I say and think that if he were closer to me I'd reach out and touch him to make a point, but he's farther down the beach. "And, p.s., I'm cold."

"Gotcha. This will be finished in a minute—sort of. I think personal finance issues go on forever. But anyway, so it wasn't like I was trying to deceive you by being this country bumpkin. I just didn't know what to do myself, so it came out funny with you."

"You were basically trying on the poor life?"

"Not at all—and I'll try not to be offended by that remark. But when I left Harvard—or rather, took a leave of absence to find out what the real world was like—my father, in typical uptight fashion, decided to take away any money I had."

"But aren't you eighteen? Can he do that?"

"Until I'm twenty-five, he controls the funds. It's how it's always been in the Addison family. Like at twenty-five you magically know what's right and what's wrong."

"So . . ." I say. "What a long and illuminating evening."

"It's the shortest night, Love," Charlie says, and then puts the piece of driftwood into the wet sand. "There."

"What's there?"

"That," Charlie says and rests his hand on top of the marker, "is where we are now."

"And where is that, exactly?" I ask. I put one foot in front of the other and take careful steps closer to him.

"Here," Charlie says, and right when I think he'll lean down and kiss me, he points to the small cabin and gestures us both inside.

It's funny to look at something from the outside—like this cabin when I first drove off the ferry and followed Charlie's red pickup here—and then to find yourself inside, like I am now.

"So this is yours?" I ask and look around the open-plan room. To the left is a small kitchen (note: it's clean with no dishes in the sink), to the right, a big stone fireplace, and in front, all windows lined with one long cushioned seat—the perfect spot to sit and gaze out at the beach, which the windows overlook.

"Yes and no," Charlie says as he piles logs into the empty fireplace and hands me some newspaper. "Here—twist and crumple."

I start to unfold the paper, crumpling a couple of sheets into balls, and another few into folded fanlike lengths that I twist and hand to Charlie, who sets them inside his wood pile. "Hey, we make a good team." Hey—I sound idiotic! Leave it to me to feel all windswept and adult making a fire in a cabin with a boy I like who might like me and ruin the moment by adding some generalized, sports-influenced rah-rah shit.

But Charlie doesn't comment on this. Instead, he lights a match, starts the fire, and asks, "So what's the deal with you and Henry, anyway?"

Oh—not expecting that one. I warm my hands near the flames to buy a second or two to think. "Truth?" I ask, and Charlie nods, his tongue in the side of his cheek. "Nothing."

"So back rubs on the beach are nothing? Just your standard summer fling summer fun . . ."

"Are you spying on me? I don't know whether to be freaked out or flattered."

"Mike saw you with Henry—and since she's been down that road before . . ."

"What road is that, exactly?"

"The Henry Randall all women are mine road," Charlie says.

"Oh," I say, noncommittal. I mean, clearly Charlie and Henry have a little guy competition thing going on, and though it's easy to see Henry as a player, a high roller on the hookup table of craps even, it's not the way I saw him. Then again, I've been wrong before. "Well, I guess I've, uh, strayed from that path. Or road. Or highway."

Charlie opens a kitchen cabinet, reaching high up and re-vealing a bit of skin underneath his untucked white shirt. In my mind, I'm drooling, but exteriorly, I manage to stay calm.

"Red or white?" Charlie asks.

I think for a second. Not sure wine is going to do me any

favors with my shift tomorrow, my fairly empty stomach, and my need to keep my wits about me. "Neither, thanks."

"Okay, not red . . ." Charlie decides and instead of handing me a glass, tucks something into his pocket and walks right to me. His eyes lock with mine, and then in one smooth motion he puts one arm around my waist, the other around my shoulders, and kisses me. I kiss back with all the feelings of lust and crush I've had building up. When we stop for a second, Charlie hands me something. "If not red or white, how about blue and white . . ."

I look at the object in my hand. "Oh—not red wine. Okay. Feeling cool." The mug fits perfectly in my palm, despite its lack of handle. I grip it as though there's a cup of coffee inside. "I can't believe you have this! I've been semi-obsessive about looking for it."

"Who'd you think had it?"

I lean back on the kitchen counter, my elbows resting on the edge. "I have no idea, but I guess I thought . . ."

"It'd be with someone more important?" Charlie half grins at me. "Here, this is the note that goes with it."

"No, not important, just . . ." Maybe more of a key player in my life. But maybe this is what Mable's trying to tell me. The scroll he hands me is tied with a pink ribbon, a reminder of Mable's fight. I untie the bow and unfurl the letter that is a continuation of the note I found at Tink's pottery place.

> "Find the matching blue and white mug and drink in all life has to offer. Everyone deserves a . . .

> Second chance. Even when life—or love—or the poten-
> tial for it—comes to pieces, it doesn't mean the
> shards should be thrown away. Some of the best rela-
> tionships are those that are salvaged."

I wonder if this is Mable's way of hinting that she should have repaired things with my mother—Gala—a long time ago. Or if she lost love and wished she reclaimed it. I keep reading.

> "I spent some time with Charlie this winter and spring
> when I visited, and he's a stand-up guy. A gorgeous,
> funny, stand-up guy who likes you—a lot. But you
> needed to find this out for yourself. If you're reading
> this, then you have. Now go and find the meaning of
> your name. Oh—and if you're looking for your next clue,
> you'll have to search high and low. XXs forever, Mable."

I blush when I read the part about Charlie being so good-looking, which of course he is, but I am really glad that I chose to read the note silently rather than out loud. When I'm done, I roll it back up, slide the ribbon back on, and say, "Mable wanted me to give you a second chance. You know, after the diner disaster . . ."

"She told me I could give you the mug whenever I first saw you, but I wanted to wait. To make sure . . ."

"To make sure what? That I was worth the trouble?" I smile at him and reach out for his jacket lapels, using them to pull him closer to me.

"Something like that. Plus . . ." Charlie stops for a second, looks away, and then looks back at me, choosing his words carefully. "There've been a lot of girls—oops, that doesn't sound good." I laugh but wait to see where this is headed. "A lot of people like the idea of money. Or the perception of my money. Which is just ironic because I don't have any to speak of now . . ."

"Well, your background—financially speaking—is impressive," I say and watch his face fall slightly. "It's impressive, but I'm not impressed with it." I take a breath and a risk. "But I'm kind of impressed with you . . ."

Cue the stringed instruments or the cool offbeat soundtrack by an indie film producer (oh—like Martin Eisenstein!) as we kiss and connect, with the straps of my borrowed dress sliding slightly off my shoulders, Charlie's jacket in a heap on the floor, and my heart soaring.

"So you're cool with thinking of me as just a boat bum?" Charlie asks.

"If that's how you want it, sure. And what about me?"

"What about you?" he asks, his eyes glazed over with that guy look they get when they're struggling to pay attention to words due to booty beckoning.

"How do you want to see me?" I put my hands flat on his chest.

"Exactly as you are. A woman with a lot to say—who's perfect for me."

And we leave it at that, kissing, talking, and hanging out in the small beach cottage until the sun rises and he drives me back home.

A few days later, in the new-relationship phase that clouds my vision, mind, and mouth (I keep flipping words and letters and appear perpetually tongue-tied), Charlie invites me to do the most romantic thing:

"You want me to clean your boat?" I ask, and sound thrilled despite the Cinderella-style date. It's the first time he's asked me onboard—the bleach and water combo is an added bonus.

"So if you scrub like this"—Charlie reaches underneath one of the built-in seats with a wet sponge—"you can get more bang for your buck."

"Oh," I say, semidrooling over the grungy-fisherman thing he has going—all faded and cutoff khakis and a shirt so threadbare it betrays the definition of clothing. "Can we have one of those stereotypical movie moments, where the guy teaches the girl a new trade—say welding or something . . . ?"

Charlie picks up my lead. "Or golfing, where the guy has to stand behind the girl . . . like this?" He comes over so his chest is pressed to my back and repeats the scrubbing demo with the sponge. "Better?"

I turn back to see his face without moving apart from his grip. "Perfect," I say, and we stay like that, washing the boat and talking until the inside and the outside (which we cleaned with long-handled brushes) are frothy.

"Can I interest you in a shower?" Charlie asks.

"Ahem?" I say as a word, not a cough.

"No—not that kind. This kind." Charlie unrolls a coiled hose and hands the spout to me. "I'll go turn it on, you wash it down."

It's therapeutic, actually, spraying all the sludge and fishy smells and bleach off, leaving a shiny clean boat.

"Now, if you really wanted to live the cliché, this is where I'd spray you, and you'd giggle and then I'd just happen to get your T-shirt wet . . ." Charlie says as I hand him back the hose.

"Yeah, and then I'd be all wet and overtly vixeny and then you'd go to kiss me and my dad would show up."

Charlie considers all this. "That sounded great up until the last part . . ."

I reach for his hand. "Well, you don't have to worry—my dad's not here. However, I'm not planning on being hosed down, either."

"How about just getting a sandwich, then?" he asks and points to the diner where he stood me up so long ago. "Proof we're past it?"

"Lead the way." I nod—and he does.

Chapter 12

"Are you sure I'm not going to be late?" I ask Charlie for the second time. The day has flown by—literally. His buddy, Chet, owns a plane, and we went for an aerial tour of the island with Arabella this morning. She then went back to work at the café and I'm due for the evening shift. I left my watch at the tiny airport, so now my wrist feels naked and my panic about being late has crept in.

"You'll be fine," Charlie says. "You don't need a watch to know the time."

"Sounds like a discarded Dylan lyric," I say and for the first time in two weeks—since that night in Charlie's cabin—I think about Jacob. Not because I miss him—at least not actively. Maybe a fragment of missing him way beneath the surface. But only because of the Dylan thought. Jacob is connected to music in my mind, and therefore impossible to shake off completely.

"Anyway," Charlie says, rolling over to face me, the waves now at his back as we lie on the oversized beach blanket he keeps stored in his truck. "If you need to know the time, you can just check your front yard. Carolus Linnaeus, this Swedish botanist, observed that some flowers open at certain times. Like dandelions between five and six in the morning."

"And when do dandelions close?" I ask, half joking, and half impressed by his obscure knowledge.

Charlie squints in the bright sunlight and props his head up with one hand, tracing an invisible pattern on my bathing suit with the other. "You're testing me, but don't . . . They close at two or three, water lilies open at seven or eight and close around six or seven."

"So if I happen to remember all this and just happen to be around a flower garden, I'm all set," I say and raise my eyebrows at him. He leans down and kisses me.

"You could just do what the Romans did—"

"Dress in togas?"

"No, Love, rely on the sun. The shadow cast by a stick is shortest at noon." Charlie is so hot—or at least I find him so—that everything he does or says seems appealing. Or suggestive.

"So I need a big stick?" I ask, mentally putting my hand to my lewd mouth.

"We'll see," he says and flops back down on the blanket, the sand's heat warming us from underneath, our hands clasped together, even though they're both slightly sticky from the sunscreen.

Then I remember that I have random trivia knowledge myself. "You know, flower boy, that you can use the moon to tell time, too."

Charlie, bemused, rolls his head toward mine so we're nose

to nose. Revoltingly cute if I do say so myself. "The moon—it's highest at midnight . . ."

"Like a lot of the summer people," Chris says from above us. His body casts a shadow on us and Charlie and I laugh at his comment, then sit up to say hello.

"Hey, Chris," Charlie says, using his hand like a visor.

Chris nods hello at Charlie and then motions for me to come with him for a second.

"Back in a minute," I say to Charlie and get up, trying to fix the bathing suit wedgie I've managed to acquire.

"What's the scoop?" I ask when Chris has led me a little farther away from my comfy spot with Charlie.

"Two things," Chris says. "One—you look good in that suit. I'm glad I convinced you to buy it."

"Well, you're a shopper's best friend—truthful but tactful. What's the other thing?"

"No," Chris says and slings his towel over his shoulder. "That didn't count. That was just an aside."

"Okay—fine—what're the two things?"

Chris motions with one finger, subtly trying to guide my gaze down the beach to a large green umbrella under which Haverford Pomroy is currently engaged in reading a book. "Today's the day."

"For what?" I ask, though I have my suspicions. Chris likes Haverford so much—likes that Haverford is into sports but not a jock, into hanging out with no particular goal without being a total stoner, and of course that he's easy on the eyes.

"I can't take it anymore. I just have to know. I'm done with the guessing game of is he *huh* or not."

"Well, here's to honesty." I watch Chris's face, seeing that he's fairly calm, considering. "Not to make you nervous, but you do realize that if you do this you're potentially going to make things a little—no, a lot—tense?"

"Believe me, I get it. Not many people like being asked—even supercasually—hey, are you gay? 'Cause you seem it . . ." Chris cracks up and then stops. "But I'm just going to frame it in the context of my own feelings and see what happens. I mean, I'm leaving Friday to go back to Hadley, so what do I have to lose?"

I lift my shoulders. "You tell me."

Chris sighs. "Oh, and the other thing. You got a call from Mrs. Dandy-Patinko. She was all friendly and summer happy, but was digging about colleges."

"You mean she called only me? Or was this part of the Hadley hell—and she's phoning around to everyone with a buzz kill?"

Chris waves to Haverford, who waves back. "I didn't actually ask that. But she did happen to mention a letter she forwarded to you here."

"To the café?" I look back at Charlie and watch him watching people. I wonder if he's checking girls out or just zoning, or thinking about the future.

"No—to the post office. General delivery."

"Thanks for the message. I'll run by there before my shift . . . In my fantasy I just opened the letter and it's from some amazing school and they're begging me to go."

Chris nudges me and I nudge him back. "Yeah, right."

Chris heads off to make his proclamations and I poke my toe into Charlie's thigh. I love that I can just do that now. Two weeks ago, I couldn't look at him without blushing and no—well, now I still blush, but at least I can hold his hand when I feel like it. "Can I pick you up later tonight?"

"My shift goes until midnight," I say. "Or will you know that just by checking how high the moon is or what flower is open . . . ?"

Charlie hops up, brushes off the sand from his arms, and pulls me close. "Can I pick you up then? I know a place that's open late."

I nuzzle into him, feeling the heat emanating from his chest. "You know where to find me," I say. We kiss for a minute and then I begin the long walk back to my car, carrying my water bottle, my shoes, my bag, and my happy heart all close to me.

I notice Henry getting out of his car as I'm getting into mine. I parked next to Charlie's red pickup and if I look at it through Henry's eyes, it looks stupid. Like we're so couply we can't even park independently.

"Hey, Love," Henry says. His voice doesn't completely betray his social grace but it's lacking a certain warmth it had before (BC—before Charlie). Henry and I never spoke about the dinner party, but suffice to say from island gossip, he knows I went home with Charlie and I know he wasn't alone that night. (Mike, Charlie's sister, saw him rolling around the lawn of the Manor Club with some girl after the party had ended.)

"Hey there," I say from the distance of my car. I put the car in gear to let Henry know I'm not planning on a big-time talk.

Leaving Jay Daventree, whose white-blond hair seems iridescent in the sunlight, Henry gives me the one-minute sign so I don't peel out of the paved area. With his usual saunter, Henry walks over, his watch looking shinier than ever, his shorts with their obvious label, his car gleaming behind him. Somehow, since getting together with Charlie, who has equal—probably more—wealth but who doesn't flaunt it, I've seen Henry in a different light. He likes his labels and his "small dinner party" of course wound up being at the ritziest place on the island. And even though he's nice, I guess part of it seems like an act now. Or maybe it's real, but it's covered by the need to appear cool at all times.

"So, here long?" Henry asks, deliberately leaving out any pronoun and thus avoiding having to mention Charlie's presence.

"A couple hours," I say, not needing to shove it in his face.

"I heard you went flying today," Henry says, like it's common knowledge.

I bite my lip and put my hands on the wheel and decide to answer like it's no big deal rather than pestering him for how he knows and why he cares. "It was cool. We could see all the way to Nantucket and I thought I'd be nauseated, but I wasn't . . ."

"Did Charlie fly?" Henry's mouth is shut tightly, defiant.

I recoil a little. "No. His friend Chet did."

Henry nods. "Chet Stein. He's a good guy."

"Wow, someone who actually meets with your approval," I say and then wish I hadn't. It's just that Henry's so judgmental about Charlie, and about everything that isn't part of his perfect little world. "Sorry. Never mind."

Henry leans down so he's close to me, resting his arms on my open window. It'd be flirty if it weren't tense. Or maybe it still is but in that loaded, dramatic way. "Chet's been flying since he was nine. His mother's family owns the airport and . . ." Then he shakes his head. "I won't bore you with the details. But you should ask Charlie why he didn't take you up himself. Maybe that'll—ah—shed some light on the issue at hand."

"Okay," I say, overly friendly to show that I'm not buying into the guy battle for good versus evil and that I'm more than ready to leave. "I'll ask him."

Henry takes a step back and when he speaks, his tone is totally different, upbeat and fun like nothing just happened. "Hey, it's almost the Fourth. Got any plans?"

With the car in reverse, I lean out the window. "I'm not sure yet. It kind of depends."

I leave it open-ended, not to give the illusion of mystery and be all coy, but because I don't know. Arabella wants to get dressed up and go to the Island Ball, which Trip Randall (aka Henry's dad) throws annually. It sounds boring and expensive, but she thinks it's funny, and if we go with the right spirit it will be fun. Plus the best views of the fireworks are reported to be from their back deck. Other items on offer include making double money at the café since no one wants to work, going back to Boston to be with my dad and Louisa as they picnic by the Charles River (read: Love intrudes on a romantic evening), or asking Charlie what he's doing. I guess part of me figured he'd have told me by now if he wanted to hang out—but he hasn't brought it up.

I drive back through Katama and down to the traffic island, where I turn left and park at the shopping center. The post office is set back a bit and I flip-flop up the ramp and inside where it's cool and dark to see if there's any mail for me. Mostly I've gotten postcards from Hadley people—Harriet Walters, who is doing some journalism school; Keena Tonclair, my buddy from London, wrote to tell me about her summer breakup with my former vocal coach. She also told me about her mother's new project, a writing fellowship. I wrote back to ask more questions but haven't heard anything. The postcards have come to the café or to my house (which of course won't be my house in the fall) and my dad sent them to me in one big packet complete with the Hadley Hall crest.

But here, in the B folder of general delivery mail, I find a simple white envelope addressed to me. Back outside it's so bright I can hardly see anything, but once my eyes adjust I tear open the envelope and a letter—from Mrs. Dandy-Patinko telling me she's secured a coveted interview at Stanford with Hadley alum (and trustee) Martha Wade. Martha's the trustee everyone wants to befriend because rumor has it she can get you in—or keep you out. But when I look closely I see that the interview is next week and I don't have the cash for a ticket, nor do I have the time blocked off on my schedule at the café. Basically, I'm screwed.

I drive back slowly, in that haze of too many thoughts swirling around my already summer-dim brain. I'm zoning with the windows down, the loose chatter and ice cream crowds milling around the stop-and-go traffic in town, when I happen to look up. There, on the side of a gray-shingled building just three streets away from the café, is a small sign that reads RARE BOOKS: WHEN YOU'VE BEEN HUNTING HIGH AND LOW. Actually, the sign is so faded from years of rain, sun, and Vineyard weather that it says RARE OOKS, but I'm still of sound mind enough to know the *B* is missing.

This jolts me from my college trouble haze—Mable's note said to look high and low. With all the excitement of getting together with Charlie, of having that summer boyfriend I wanted, my treasure hunt slipped to the back of my mind. But now I wonder if this tiny upstairs bookshop is what Mable had in mind. I check my watch—if I go in now, I'll be late for my shift. And Arabella won't be happy since she worked a double. But if I don't go now I won't be able to go until tomorrow and it'll drive me crazy all night. I'm just not the most patient person in the world.

"Hey, it's me," I say into the phone.

"I can't talk—we're swamped. I'll be right there. One triple mocha no cream," she answers.

"I'll be five minutes late—is that okay? I promise I'll take over when I get there."

"I'm exhausted," Arabella moans through her teeth lest the customers hear her.

"I know, but I covered for you three days ago," I remind her. In general, we've been fine trading shifts and she's definitely helped make my hours easier so far, but in the past couple weeks I've noticed she's been grumpy about any favors I ask, but more than willing to ask me for them herself.

"Fine. Just don't be more than fifteen minutes. I have . . ."

"What?" I ask. "A hot date?"

"I gotta go," she says and shouts "double latte extra foam" before hanging up.

Maybe Arabella does have a hot date. Or maybe she's annoyed about Charlie. Or maybe it's lame that I've been sucked to the boy side. I so don't want to be that girl who drops her friends when the perfect guy comes along—but it's difficult. Charlie has weird hours from his days at the dock, I have odd hours from the shifts at Slave to the Grind II (we really need to change the name), and Arabella has equally irregular work times, too. The math involved in arranging a simple dinner or ice cream outing is astounding. So she and I have kind of been missing each other lately.

I park in my favorite spot down by the Chappaquiddick ferry, and walk past a couple of art galleries to the shingled building. Wrapped around the outside are rickety wooden steps and a wobbly railing that I grip tightly even though I doubt it would actually keep me from falling down if I tripped.

The door is red and peeling, the high and low sign swings

in the wind, tapping against the side of the building. I go inside, looking around for signs of life or of clues, but I see only
rows of books. Stacked from floor to ceiling are paperbacks,
hardcovers, beautifully bound leather dictionaries, and those
old, oversized logs that used to keep track of store tallies.
(Mable went through a phase of keeping all her books by
hand, so they look familiar.)

"Are you looking for something in particular?" asks a
woman who appears from behind a tall bookshelf.

"I'm not sure," I say. And I'm really not. It's fun to follow
Mable's map, but it's also embarrassing to put myself out there,
asking questions of people I don't know, going places I
wouldn't normally visit, and generally stretching my comfort
zone. But of course that's her point.

"We have some new arrivals," the lady says and points to a
crate of books that have yet to be arranged. She reminds me of
someone—with her gentle manner, her quiet but self-assured
way of speaking, the way she carefully examines each book before shelving it. Louisa—she reminds me of Louisa. Maybe it's
just because they both run bookstores. As I wander around the
stacks and shelves, I think of my dad with Louisa, of my life
back at Hadley. Then I try to imagine going back there, how
anxious I'll feel packing my books and clothes and heading to
the dorms this fall. In the course of three seconds I go from
missing my dad and wishing I could in fact go on a picnic with
him and Louisa for the Fourth of July to being incredibly annoyed that he's making me become a boarder after two years
of happy day-student life. My hand rests on a hardcover book

whose cover depicts a figure reaching back for a hand that isn't there.

"That's a wonderful novel," the book woman says.

I read the name *In the Midst of Ephemera* by Poppy Massa-Tonclair. PMT! My English teacher from London. "I know her!" I say and smile. It's so cool to see someone's name on a book—that is, someone with whom I actually communicate.

"Lucky you," the book woman says like she's not sure if she should believe that this random redheaded girl in fraying shorts and a bikini top would really know an award-winning author. "She's judging the Beverly William Award—but you probably knew that."

Um, no, actually I didn't, but then again news of international book awards is hardly part of my everyday summer sprawl. "Right." I nod like I know what I'm talking about and then mentally shake my head at myself. When did I become one of those people who pretends to know something when she doesn't? That's always annoyed me about other people and yet I've found myself doing it every so often to my own dismay. Why bother saying you know a certain song or like a certain book or know a political opinion when you don't? So I take it back. "I didn't know she did that. She taught me for a semester in London."

The woman smiles for real now and reaches out for the book in my hand. "I studied abroad once—a long time ago. It's such a great experience. I had the opportunity to stay on but . . ." She looks at me and shakes off her own words. "Regardless . . . would you like this book?" She opens the front cover to look at the price. "It's a first edition from the seventies."

Did I plan on buying anything in here? No, but why not? I should have PMT's books on my shelves in something nicer than my rumpled, water-stained paperbacks. "I would," I say and feel my back pocket for money. Then I have that panic you get when you know you're late. "Here—I'm sorry, I have to go. I'm late for work and . . . by the way, weird question, but do you have anything else for me? Like a note or a clue?"

I expect the woman to nod and say something like of course she does or how clever I am, but instead she hands me the book, takes my money, and looks at me like I'm crazy. Nice. I blush and accept the book and run down the rickety stairs and over to the café, where I put the book by the door to the flat and continue in my breathless pace to the counter.

Arabella wordlessly hands me an apron and I tie it around my waist. Then she points to my top, which at this point is still one half of a bathing suit. Like a scolded child, I untie the apron, run upstairs, and return with an appropriate T-shirt.

"I said ten minutes," she says while she punches out and I punch in. The crowd has thinned now after the post-lunch frenzy. The next crowd will come in in a few minutes, getting that caffeine burst before the evening kicks into gear.

"Actually, you said fifteen," I say.

"The point is, I've been working nonstop and I thought you'd be here."

"I thought you'd be here" hangs like cartoon bubble words in front of us. I make a fresh pot of coffee and make space in the cooler so it can chill afterwards while Arabella watches me, not helping at all since her shift is finished. When we first started we acted like we were one person, filling in over here, taking over over there, our skills overlapping like a piano part for four hands. But that was when serving coffee and greeting customers and refilling cream pitchers felt new and exciting. Now that the novelty has more than worn off, we're stuck in the drudgery of running a café.

"Hey, what're your plans later?" she asks.

I'm hopeful she wants to reconcile whatever rift we have happening and I'm about to say nothing when I remember Charlie's offer to swing by at midnight. "I have plans with Charlie," I say like I'm admitting to something bad.

Arabella looks at her watch. "I have to go."

"Where're you headed?" I ask and feel a dread when I think of the eight long hours I have ahead of me here.

"I'm meeting Chris," Arabella says.

I think for a second and wrinkle my mouth. "He's at the beach—with Haverford."

Arabella nods. "I know. I'm . . . we're meeting and then I'm going exploring."

Something in her tone sounds weird, but quite possibly I am on high alert because I feel guilty and bad about our lack of good vibes at the moment. "Oh, well, have fun. And feel free to stop by while I'm here."

She nods and walks the heavily traveled path from the counter to the stairs of our apartment, leaving me to deal with dishes and desserts for the afternoon's peckish people. From the back oven I take out a tray of marshmallow brownies and begin sifting their tops with graham cracker crust the way Mable taught me when she invented the s'more bars.

We used to sit on the counter at night when Slave to the Grind's doors were locked, breaking the leftover treats into bits, eating them with our fingertips. She talked about how happy the café made her—and I guess I thought it would make me happy, too. She made café life appear so easy, but I'm learning that things look easy when they're fun or you're good at it or you just have a goal to succeed. Where do I find that in my own life?

Chapter 13

I slice the s'more bars into squares, place them on platters, and add them to the items for sale in the confectioner's corner when it hits me: I feel happiest when I'm writing. Not just in my journal—but anywhere. Give me a pen and a piece of paper, a keyboard and a screen, chalk and pavement, and I'm golden. Singing is great—I like that, too—but the songwriting part is what hooked me. The words. Connecting phrases and ideas and turning them into one whole story. I'm hit with a movie reel of images from my past—jotting entries in my journals, sitting with Poppy Massa-Tonclair in her office and the incredible feelings I had then of writing a twenty-five-page essay for Brit Lit and getting an A because I worked hard and because it meant something to me, and how I avoided writing a big creative project this spring because part of me couldn't accept being so invested in something. But I am. I look around for someone to tell, someone with whom I can share my good news of self-revelation, but there's no one here except a few customers.

The café phone rings.

"Slavetothegrindtwo," I say as all one word. Note to self: Must get new name for this place. It's a mouthful and then some.

"It's just me."

"Hey, Chris," I say and then remember he might have news to share. "So what happened? Was it a love connection with Haverford?"

"Not exactly . . ." he says.

"Where are you? There's so much noise in the background."

"I'm . . . listen, I'm heading back early to Hadley."

"But what about the Fourth of July? Not to guilt trip you into staying, but what could possibly be enticing about being back on campus?"

"The ferry's leaving in ten minutes. Just keep my stuff and I'll get it in a few weeks. I just need to get back on track."

"Why, were you derailed?" I ask.

"Let's just say that Haverford threw me for a loop."

I bite my lip in sympathy. "Why? Did you ask the *huh* question and get a negative response?"

"Not exactly. I have to go, though. You can reach me at the dorm—sucks for me, but I'll be living there while planning the all-new gay-straight-lesbian-transgender alliance. Par-ty!"

"You'll make it great, I'm sure. But don't you dare leave me in the lurch about Haverford. Is he gay or what?"

The ferry's horn blows in the background, so Chris shouts. "Yup—he's gay. But the crappy part? He's already seeing someone."

"So it's a summer fling, right? It'll be over by the time school starts . . ." I say it about Haverford and whoever his male hottie is, but maybe I'm also thinking about Charlie and me. The trouble with summer things or summer flings is that you're supposed to relish them while they're in season and then let them fade like a tan. But what if you like the person too much?

"No, Love, you're not getting it. Haverford's been seeing Ben Weiss this whole time."

"Ben Weiss as in—in our class at Hadley? As in jocky Ben Weiss who did that lunchroom thing last year?"

"The one and only. I thought the worst reaction from Haverford would be shock at my assuming he could be gay or bi. But you know what? It's so much worse to find out that he is, um, in my league, but yet totally out of it. Straight means he rejected a whole population. Gay means he just rejected me."

"I'm sorry," I say and flip the brew switch off on the decaf. "I know how much you liked him."

"Like him," Chris corrects. "Not liked. It's still in the present."

"Talk soon?"

"Yeah," he says. "Maybe my pride'll be mended enough by August to come back for Illumination Night."

"That's a month from now," I whine.

"I know—later."

I hang up and walk around to each table refilling sugar canisters, plumping pillows, and wondering about love. How one person can be so alluring it's hard to imagine they don't feel the same way toward you. This makes me think of Jacob, who is probably off somewhere wooing the women of Europe. No—wait—he's doing college tours. So he could be . . . wait. Why do I care?

I can see the throngs of coffee consumers casually winding their way up the street and back, browsing the shops of Edgartown and inevitably heading my way, but since I've swept, prepared the baked goods, and topped off the water pitchers, I go ahead and call home.

"Dad, guess what?" I ask.

"You're in Spain," he says and I can't see his face to know what fraction is a joke and what's genuine concern.

"Do you really think I'd head out of the country without telling you first?" I ask and then silently debate the merit of my question.

"I hope not," Dad says, which tells me he wouldn't put it past me. This of course makes me think he doesn't entirely trust me, which pisses me off, dampening my excitement a little.

"Well, I'm still on the Vineyard. But I have news . . ." I want to tell him about my writing revelations.

"I'll be right there!" he shouts, though not to me, and then adds, "Louisa and I are climbing a mountain today . . ."

"How von Trapp. Isn't it a little late in the day for hiking?" I ask and go on automatic as I steam milk and ring up sales.

"It's only at Blue Hills. She's planned a special picnic."

I raise my eyebrows like my dad can see this across the

phone wires. "You guys are all about the picnics these days, huh?"

"I guess . . . So, what's your big announcement?" Dad taps his pen against the phone, one of his habits.

I take a breath and want to tell him about writing—but then I feel dumb, like it's one of those announcements a little girl might say to her imaginary friends at a tea party. "I'm going to be a princess" or something. "Nothing," I say. "Really. I just wanted to say hi."

That's the thing about life goals—if you talk about them too much and then change your mind, you just look foolish. And I don't want to do that, to be a punch line.

"Oh," Dad answers. "I thought maybe you were calling to ask for money."

"Why would you think that?"

"Because you haven't so far, and I ran into Dorothy Dandy-Patinko and of course she shared the news about your Stanford interview . . ."

My hopes climb up as Dad talks. He'll just get the plane ticket for me. No big deal. "It would be really great if you could help with that. I mean, it's a college expense, right?"

Dad coughs and is quiet. A customer looks annoyed at me that I have yet to produce a shot of vanilla espresso. "The truth of it is, Love, that I'm less than keen for you to go to California."

"For the interview?" I ask and hand the espresso to the man, who skulks off.

"For anything. It's too far for college. How would I visit with the Hadley terms and . . . ?"

"So you're saying I can't even apply to schools out there?"

"What does the West Coast have that Boston, Providence, New York, DC, or Vermont can't offer you?"

I want to shout "palm trees" or something equally inane, but I'm so surprised I don't know what to say except, "You never told me I was limited geographically."

"You never asked."

"I just assumed—"

"Right. You assumed, but incorrectly. I told you this spring that I had hesitations and now, after talking it over with Louisa . . ."

"Louisa? She has no knowledge of my academic interests," I say even though it's not exactly true. She does have some idea, but the thought of her influencing my father about where I can or cannot spend four years of my life makes me so pissed off. "Even if I go to school in Connecticut or someplace, it doesn't mean I'll be running home every two seconds."

"But you could," Dad says. "And that's the difference."

I think for a second, the anger and frustration building in me until I have heartburn. "You're so contradictory, Dad. You're making me board at school when I could be living at home with you for the last time and yet you won't let me really go off on my own! California or Connecticut makes no difference—you have to let go at some point."

I want him to say that I'm correct, that of course he has to let go and that maybe he'll reconsider the dorm issue for the fall, but he doesn't. "Love, I want you to be happy. But I want you to spread your wings with the knowledge that being part of a small, untraditional family has its own constraints."

"What's that supposed to mean?" I slick the marble counter with a damp rag, wiping it free of crumbs and coffee rings.

"It means . . . I give you permission to go to California, but I don't like the idea. And I'm realizing that despite our fairly good dynamic, I need to institute some limitations. I let you go to the Vineyard by yourself at age seventeen with no supervision. Don't think for a second I don't understand what that entails . . . but in terms of funding a cross-country trip that could very well lead to hardly seeing you? Forget it."

"So I'm on my own," I say, my voice flat.

"I'm more than happy to pay for a regional tour and any expenses therein." Dad's words have started to sound like catalogue copy for a prep school—which I guess he basically is.

"You know what?" I stack steaming coffee mugs straight from the dish dryer, not wincing even though they're hot. "Don't pay for anything." I think of Charlie and how he allowed himself to be cut off from his family's money so he could do what he wanted. "I'll pay for it all. I don't know how, but I will. And that way, since I'm responsible for it all, I can say what I do. Sound fair?"

Dad swallows and sighs. "It sounds reasonable." Then, like we weren't just disagreeing, he switches to cheerful mode. "Well, we're off for an evening hike. And remember, I'm out of town from the sixth onward."

"Right. How could I forget your culinary tour through Sardinia . . . ?"

Something I have to get used to is my "emergency contact person." It used to be if Dad went out of town I could always rely on Mable if I needed anything. Of course I'm older, I can drive, and I have a semidecent idea of how the world works (most of the time), but what if I needed someone? Who would I call? I never really thought about this that much, having been part of a strong twosome (Dad and me) and a triangle of support (me, Dad, Mable). This thought leads me directly to thoughts of Gala—who exists somewhere—not that she'd be my emergency contact person necessarily, but she could feature in my life, right? I say her name in my head as I work, counting out my hours with coffees served, like T. S. Eliot talked about in his poetry. So much for feeling elated about writing. It's not as though words are going to magically whisk me to California, to my interview, to the infamous Eisenstein party in Malibu on July third, to anywhere, really. So I suck it up and keep working, my mind—and my coffee—brewing.

Chapter 14

I always hated those movie scenes where the main character—usually the heroine (save for the *Risky Business* antics of *that* male lead)—decides to dance around in either (a) her underwear (b) her bedroom (c) the school cafeteria (d) a public place like a mall, or (e) her place of employment. She just sheds her inhibitions and quite possibly her clothing and suddenly bursts into song. It's the movie way of either showing how cool the star is underneath that drab exterior or showcasing her hidden talent for song, or—and this is what I despise the most—setting her up for some big embarrassing moment whereby her crush or prom date or supercool employer catches her in the act and she's all openmouthed and blushing.

But despite the fact that I loathe these scenes, I manage to create one just for myself. Eleven at night two days pre–Fourth of July and no one seems to desire a cup of anything remotely related to coffee, unless it's coffee-flavored vodka shots, and since Slave to the Grind II doesn't have a liquor license, that's not an option. Suffice to say I am without customers and without motivation to do anything else but close up early. So I do

my usual counter cleanup, switching off all the machines, setting up for the morning shift, and place the upturned chairs on
the café tables so I can mop. Of course my mop turns into a
microphone and then morphs into a dance partner as I glide
effortlessly around the café, swashing tepid water along the
checkered floor as I belt out the lamest possible songs from the
series of CDs Mable gave me a couple of years ago.

At the top of my vocal range I croon Air Supply's "All Out
of Love" (even though I'm not—thankfully!) and Dionne
Warwick's "That's What Friends Are For." I'm midway through
the musical tribute to being a good buddy when I hear a tell-
tale flop 'n' flip from Arabella's shoes and sure enough she's
standing there watching me perform my act with the mop.

"Yes, folks, I do need a life," I say and add, "This is just like
those terrible scenes in movies . . ."

Arabella smiles at me enough so I'm pretty sure she's
walked off her pissy mood from before. In fact, rather than
walking off her mood, I'd say she ballroom danced her way to
uplifted spirits: clad in a beige silk camisole and matching
tulip-shaped skirt, and adorned with several strands of long
beads, she looks dressed for an elegant evening, not a romp
around town with Chris as she'd stated before. But I don't
want to bug her by probing about her outfit's appropriateness,
so instead I offer her the mop as both an apology for our ear-
lier interaction and a chance not to be alone in my silly
songstress mode.

Arabella accepts the microphone and slides her arm over
my shoulder. I can smell wine or some other alcohol on her

breath, and she sways like she's both into the music and a little drunk, or maybe both. *"That's what friends are for . . ."* she sings.

"Keep smiling, keep . . ." I sing and then ask her, "Is it shining? I never know what she says after that . . ."

Arabella laughs, which makes me laugh, and it dawns on me how long it's been since we've been just the two of us, no guys, just having a ridiculous time together. "It might be shimmying. No, that wouldn't fit . . ." She looks around and says, "I'm glad you're closing up. It'll give us a chance to have a conference upstairs."

Her arm is still around me and I don't want to break the mood by telling her I expect Charlie any second. "You look really nice, by the way." I don't ask her why; I just wait to see if she offers up any info.

"Thanks," Arabella says and looks down at her silky outfit half surprised to find she's wearing it. "I had a dinner."

I give her my "spill it" look, but she doesn't take the cue. And right now it feels more important to get back on the friendship track than it does to pry. "Keep singing, Dionne."

"Why, I thought you'd never ask," she says and croons, *"Keep smiling, keep whatevering . . ."*

"Knowing you can always count on me—for sure . . ." I sing, and then we join together for the last line, singing with our hard-core-ballad faces on, all crunched up and dramatic. At which point applause echoes throughout the room.

"Bravo, encore!" Charlie commands as he claps and nods, his tongue tracing the edges of his white teeth. How anyone could be near him and not have their pulse react is beyond me.

Arabella and I bow. "Want to come upstairs for a night-cap?" she asks and takes off her embroidered flip-flops.

Charlie looks to me for an answer. I'm torn. But I know he's planned something for tonight and I haven't seen him all day. "Stay here," I tell him. "I'll be right down." I follow Arabella upstairs and begin flinging my coffee-stained T-shirt off while simultaneously trying to fluff my hair out from its pony-tail. I pull on slim-fitting navy blue pants, my go-anywhere red slides, and a tightish white long-sleeve scoop-neck T-shirt. Judging from how Charlie was dressed—not in his typical denim—I'm eschewing my love for my old khakis and trying for a bit more sophistication. Plus, the white shirt highlights my cleavage (in the good way, not the cover-of-a-guy-mag slutty way).

"Are you in for the night?" I ask Arabella.

"I am. I was hoping you would be, too. I came back early from—I came back to hang out. You know, it's not as if we've had much time together in a while."

"Yeah, I know. But let's make time. How about tomorrow?"

"I'm working, then I have a windsurfing lesson."

I raise my palms in surprise. "You're windsurfing?"

"I learned that summer I spent in Cornwall, when I met Toby, but I'm out of practice. So I'm brushing up." She flexes her arm. "It's good for the upper body. What about the next day?"

"I'm working—and I'll probably try to pull a double. I need the money."

"Oh," Arabella says, and doesn't ask me why I need the money so badly. Even though she's gotten into working this summer and earning money where she never really has before, she doesn't get what it means to truly not be able to afford something. To really have things—either material objects or goals—out of reach. Arabella hands me her tinted lip balm and watches me slide a fingertip of it onto my lips. I look in the mirror. Not the best, not the worst. It'll do. "What about the Fourth of July?"

"What about it?" I ask. "I thought you were doing the glam thing."

"Please come," she says. "Please? It'll be so silly and we'll just dress up and be funny and giggle. And watch fireworks."

"But it's at Henry's house," I say. "And he . . . we haven't really seen much of each other lately." As though that explains the tension, the snippy attitudes he and I have exchanged.

"Meaning?"

"Meaning I can't bring Charlie."

"I thought he hadn't asked you to do anything."

"Thanks for that reminder," I say and cross my arms over my chest. "He hasn't. But I'm hoping . . ." I look at my friend's face, how disappointed she looks. "I miss you, too, you know."

She hugs me and then lets out a big "Ugh. Are we too girly, or what?"

"Pathetic." I agree, and she fixes my hair because she always does and I walk to the door. "Okay."

"Okay, what?" she asks.

"Okay, I'll go to Trip Randall's big bash on the Fourth. But only because you're my best friend and it's important to you."

"It's my first American Fourth of July—I want it to be special."

"It will be," I say and feel like I've made the right choice, even though I'd rather be in a sweatshirt eating hotdogs and watching from the pier like everyone else. "Are you sure you're okay here by yourself?"

Arabella seems to blush a little, but maybe it's just the wine in her hand. "I'll be fine. Go enjoy your midnight rendezvous with Prince Charlie."

Of course, he's not a prince, but he treats me royally. Even as I think this I want to gag at my own mushiness.

We're going to live sappily ever after, I think as Charlie and I walk down the cobblestone street toward the harbor.

"Don't ruin it," I remind myself. "I'm self-conscious enough as it is."

"Just where are you taking me, anyway?" I ask and feel like a fairy tale girl, Little Red Riding Hood or something—minus the always creepy element of a witch, a wolf, or a poisoned apple.

"Can you ever just wait and see?" Charlie asks. He holds my hand; our fingers are interlaced and he pulls me around a corner and up a small path.

"What is this place?" I ask and let go of his hand so I can stop and smell the roses—literally—that flank the walls of the garden path. The narrow passageway leads us up from the street and the harborside to a set of stone steps into which a metal railing is set.

"Hold on as you climb—it makes it easier," Charlie says, walking in front of me and then waiting. "Do you want to lead?"

It could be a loaded question: Do I want to take the figurative reins of the relationship. "Do I want to make all the decisions?" I ask, slightly winded from the steep steps and steady pace.

"No. I meant, do you want to go in front of me? That way, if you fall, I can catch you."

Talk about words that sound like cheesy love songs that make me swoon regardless. "Sure. I'll go first. As long as it's not just an excuse to look at my ass."

Charlie cocks his head to one side and smiles in the moonlight. "That, too."

We keep climbing, the steps winding around the hillside until they stop at an arched wooden doorway painted black but peeling. "Here we are."

I step back and realize the door is attached to a small squat house right next to a lighthouse whose signal circles round and round, casting a sheath of light onto the grass, the steps, the water below, and then back again.

"Come on in," Charlie says. The house is vacant and I'm suddenly a little freaked out. Charlie wasn't the most upfront about being Mr. Money, who's to say he isn't hiding something else up his sleeve—like a knife. Okay, so maybe it was a mistake for me to go see that creepy movie with Chris last weekend while Arabella did God knows what at some bonfire on the beach.

"Are you secretly a slasher?" I ask.

"Yes." Charlie nods. "You've found me out." He holds his hand out to me so I'll follow him up through a strange little doorway, and the minute my hand is back in his, all traces of freaky nerves disappear. "Only one more set of stairs—I promise."

The stairwell is ancient and tiny, with sloping risers and whitewashed stone walls. Once we're at the top, we go through yet another arch and then—

"Oh, Charlie, it's so great! Oh—and the . . . and it's . . ." Watch as Love loses her language skills and instead opts for ogling. The steps led us from the keeper's house over to the actual lighthouse, and the room we're in is the top floor. Circular, with stone walls, the room is set with a long table on top of which is a stunning variety of desserts.

"You said you like sweets so . . ." He motions for me to check out the goods.

Not that the food in front of me is superfriendly to a good bathing-suit body nor is it at all necessary, but it's so, well, sweet. "You didn't have to."

Charlie goes to the far side (okay, not a side—I did get an A in geometry—but the far rim of the circle) of the room and lifts up the top of a wooden chest. "Why do you always think things are done out of necessity? Of course I didn't have to drag you all the way to a lighthouse and I didn't have to ask Paula Flan to make all this stuff . . . but I did it because it's fun. It's different."

It *is* fun, it *is* different—and it's also pretty extravagant. I could fly to California and back several times from the looks of the spread, unless Charlie managed to whip this idea all up himself—which, though he's a talented, industrious guy, I seriously doubt. But I try not to let my lurking financial fiascoes pull me away from the moment.

From the chest, I watch Charlie take out several blankets, a white comforter that seems to expand when he shakes it, and a couple of pillows. I want to ask him if this is his lair, if he brings all his women here and woos them with sugar until their brains malfunction and they agree to whatever blanket-fest he has in mind. But I don't. "Paula Flan made these?"

I investigate the food further. Chocolate ganache torte sprinkled with candied lavender; white-chocolate-covered cashews, tiramisu, oversized brownies, and good old-fashioned chocolate chip cookies. I choose one from a silver tray and take a bite. "Paula Flan, as in chef to the stars? Paula Flan who's in the papers every two seconds for her desserts? I feel humbled to eat one."

"I should've known you'd go for the ccc's," Charlie says, still arranging blankets. "Those I could make myself . . ."

"I always thought it was funny that her name is Flan and she's a baker. Granted she's like the baking mogul, but still . . ."

"You think it's destiny, with a name like that?" Charlie asks, and comes over to the table. He dips a finger into the chocolate fondue and brings it to me to lick off. Yum. Food and love—perfect combo.

"Could be. I mean, it's not like she became a lawyer. That wouldn't be funny."

Charlie thumbs to the cozy area he's set up, all layers of quilts and pillows, and I take my shoes off so I can pad onto it and sit with my next round of treats. "Following that logic, you could say I'm destined for a life of financial investing." I raise my eyebrows. "It sounds boring just saying it, let alone doing it. How all the Addisons tolerated doing the same thing for so many generations is beyond me."

"And I guess I'd wind up being . . ." I shrug and wipe the corners of my mouth lest I get choco grime in there. "A schoolmaster?" I can't help but laugh. "Definitely not."

"Bukowski . . . sounds more like you're headed for the literary realm."

I swallow my bite of pastry and look around for water. Of course, Charlie's thought of this and produces a bottle of sparkling water. I pretend to examine the contents. "This isn't spiked, is it?"

Charlie lifts himself up into a squatting position and looks at me, half smirking and half serious. "Wait. Don't gloss over the writing thing. You might be able to hide from other people . . . but under your hot redheaded exterior . . ." He thinks I'm hot! I've never been called hot—maybe pretty or attractive, but I'm not the typical hottie—so even though my self-esteem doesn't depend on that, it's still nice to hear. "Under this"—Charlie touches my hair and puts it behind my shoulders—"is a real writer, I think."

I shake my head. "How do you know? We hardly . . ."

"When we first hung out you told me very clearly about your journals, your songwriting, your love of books . . . even your lists of words you like and hate. That's language, that focus on words is something a writer does."

"So you don't think I'm destined to be a pop star or something?" I ask and tilt my head and mime singing into my dessert.

"I didn't buy that rock star thing for a second. You're way too academic for that. How many people go from Hadley Hall to superstardom?"

"Probably not many over the years—but there's nothing saying I couldn't be the first." I put my unfinished treat onto a white plate and wipe my hands on a napkin. Charlie pours some of the sparkling water into a glass and I sip it like it is spiked with something even though it's plain.

"Oh, and as for that other comment about me spiking the water?"

I smile over the rim of my glass. "I was just kidding."

"In every joke there's an element of truth, right?" Charlie removes his shoes, pulls off his guy-comfy gray sweater, revealing a slightly fitted waffle-knit shirt underneath. Even though it's summer, the Vineyard nights are cool. I'm chilled, too, and Charlie pulls back the puffy comforter and wordlessly suggests I get underneath. When I stay still he shakes his head, grinning. "Look, under no circumstances am I trying to seduce you."

I look at the table of delights back to the nest (read: bed) he's made and raise one eyebrow at him. It's a thing I've always been able to do—and I taught Arabella even though it's an inherited trait (a useless show of genetics, but still). As I do it, I instantly think that Mable couldn't do it, my Dad couldn't do it, and that maybe it's something my mother does. Maybe I have gestures or tastes from her and I don't even know it. "Between the bed and the brownie booty, you could've fooled me."

Charlie lies back on the blanket, his frame contrasting against the pure whiteness of it like he's in snow. On my knees, I make my way over to him—not under the covers (as if this proves anything) but next to him so I can bend down and kiss him. He breaks away for a second to tell me, "I didn't plan this night as a question."

I sit on my butt, knees up, hair semiblocking my eyes, and consider this. "You mean, this isn't a *will you*?"

"Right."

"So what is it?" I feel small, tucked into a tiny lighthouse, away from the island, the vast harbor, snug in containment.

"It's just a night," he says. Like his name is just a name, like a kiss is just a kiss, and so on.

We kiss more, and then slide under the duvet, its weight giving me warmth and a cover for my own shyness. It's not like I'm a prude and it's not as though I'm rushing to remove my wardrobe, but it feels good to cuddle with him. Or maybe cuddle is too tame. But *hook up* doesn't tell you anything; it doesn't describe any feeling—and there are feelings there. I look at Charlie and smile as he takes his shirt off. He looks at me and kisses just under my jawline. "Who needs Fourth of July fireworks, huh?" Then a blush overtakes his cheeks and he looks away. "I can't believe how corny that sounded. It was much better in my head."

"That's like how I draw—in my mind it's a perfect charcoal rendition of a figure and then on paper it's all stick figures and smudged lines."

When we're all coiled up together, limbs twisted and tangled but not entirely undressed or anything, Charlie says, "Actually, I take back what I said before. I did ask you here for a reason."

"Oh—now we get to the truth?" I debate momentarily whether I should tell him my lack of sex experience or if he's figured that out by now. But Charlie's not talking about all things physical.

"I was . . . I'm hoping you'll come with me . . ."

Our faces are so close he looks fuzzy, his eyes melding into one Cyclops eye, so I back up for a second. "Where?" I ask, even though I feel fairly certain I'd go anywhere with him or that he'd make any place better.

"To my house."

"The cottage? Now?" I sit up so he knows I'm game.

He gently pushes me back so I'm flat on the blanket again. "Not my little hovel. My other house—that's not really mine. My parents' house."

"You're inviting me home?" I ask, happy and smug.

"It's annoying," Charlie promises. "It's formal." He says it like *formal* means *smelly*. "It's all class and conformity and confinement." Then he sighs. "Home sweet home."

"It sounds fun," I say, even though what he's described isn't fun. "You know what I mean, right? Seeing where someone comes from or meeting their friends or family—it's revealing. In a good way."

"Yeah. Plus we can run around on the back lawn with multicolored sparklers."

Sparklers. Fireworks. "Wait, is this a Fourth of July thing?"

Charlie looks up at the ceiling. "Yup. The annual Addison banquet."

"I thought Trip Randall cornered the market on annual Fourth of July bashes," I say and picture Henry and his haughty crew.

Charlie sits up and turns his head over his shoulder so he can see me. "The Randalls are new money compared to us. It's lame to even say that, but it's true. And the Addisons are old, old money."

"You talk like you're not a part of it."

Charlie shrugs. "Probably because that's how I feel. Anyway, every year since the island was settled, the Addisons—"

"Your family," I add to make a point. You can't choose your family, but it's yours whether you like it or not.

"Every year *my* family invites the crustiest of the crust to this dinner. It's a thing—you know—to be invited. And the first summer Trip Randall was here—I was little, maybe five or something—he came over to the house uninvited and basically demanded to be included in the dinner."

"But he wasn't?"

"No. Not for any reason other than my parents hardly knew him. They'd mainly heard about how he was buying up all the old beach cottages and razing them so he could build mammoth summer houses and sell them for a massive profit."

"So now it's what, like a feud?"

"Pretty much. If you get invited to the Addisons', you go. God, that sounds so pretentious. Sorry. But it's just what people do. Mable went last summer."

My reaction: agog at the idea. I'm shocked. "But she's hardly rolling in it . . ." I catch myself using the present tense. "She wasn't wealthy . . ."

"You don't have to be wealthy to be invited, just interesting. So will you come? It's not like I'm close with them—my family—but I'd like to go this year. And bring you."

"So I can meet them?"

"That, plus I have an announcement to make and I want you there for it."

Cue the big drums—an announcement! "What kind?"

"Ah, not so fast. You have to come to the dinner and then you'll know."

The moment of truth. How to tell Charlie about Arabella's need to have me be with her on the Fourth. "It all sounds really good, Charlie. Really . . . I want to go . . . but I promised Arabella I'd be with her."

"She can come, too." Charlie looks worried for a second, making me think he's saying we can come, but maybe it's a slightly larger deal than he's making it out to be. Maybe he has to approach his parents at their respective thrones or something.

"She already RSVP'd to somewhere else," I say and try to avoid eye contact for a second to lessen the blow.

"Let me guess. She's going to the Randalls'—with Henry—and you're supposed to tag along?"

I'm a little disgruntled with the tagalong implications. "I am friends with them. I wouldn't be tagging along. She just wants me to spend more time with her. Which I'm sure you understand since I've been with you or working for a steady couple of weeks. It's just that . . . we planned this summer together and now . . ."

"I get it," Charlie says, his voice a little lower. He gets up and walks, shirtless, over to the sweets table and returns with a double brownie specked with caramel. "I know the value of friendship, believe me. I've misplaced a couple of friends along the way myself—or been misplaced—and I wouldn't recommend it." He doesn't elaborate on that statement, but does say, "If you can get her to change her mind . . . especially before you go . . ." Then he cuts himself off by shoving in a mouthful of brownie.

"Going? Where am I going?"

"I messed up big time—sorry. Ignore the previous comment." Charlie stands up, his mouth still crammed with chocolate, and goes to the table. "Crème brûlée."

I make a confused face, my upper lip twisted up in a statement of disbelief. "Crème brûlée? It is my favorite dessert, but its relevance to the conversation could be debated . . ."

"I know. It's your favorite, and you were supposed to go for it first, but you didn't because you're unpredictable. It's one of the things I find so appealing about you, but . . ."

"So what does it mean?"

"It means . . . eat it."

I stare at the oval ramekin and know that with the cookies,

brownie, and pastry already consumed there's no way I'm going for the binge of digesting more. "I can't. Seriously."

"Okay, fine. It's my fault anyway." Carefully, he lifts off the crunchy sugar glaze in one sheet. Underneath, in delicate icing it reads:

High calorie, get it?

I look at Charlie. "There's another note under the vegetable platter," he explains.

I look at the table. "I didn't even notice the veggies what with all the other delectables . . ."

"Keep reading."

I do.

> Searching high and low, right? High calorie, low
> calorie . . . not that you usually get consumed with
> calories or anything, but since you're headed to the
> place of vanity I figured I'd try to out-clever myself . . .
> You're the sweetest girl (even more than the crème)
> ever and your past is solid. Now it's time to find your
> future. Your e-ticket confirmation on Jet Blue is under
> your name. As you find your wings, just remember your
> roots. Always, Mable
> P.S., to find your next clue, get on board.

"It's a flexible ticket," Charlie explains. "Mable told Paula Flan, the pastry chef, who had it all in writing. She couldn't fit the whole confirmation number in the thing . . ." He points out the ramekin.

"It's a ramekin," I say and yet again my mouth is open in surprise. "So I'm just supposed to go? It's just so weird because I have this college interview in California and I've been stressing about getting money for the ticket and my dad wouldn't pay for it and . . ." Maybe Mable wasn't planning on Stanford but on something—or someone—else.

"Slow down, take a breath. Eat a bite of brûlée."

I do, and then we kiss, and it's sweet and melty and delicious.

"So I guess I'm heading to Cali," I say, thinking of my alumni interview, the potential for starstruck stupor if I manage to get to Martin Eisenstein's party, and if all this is leading me on a bigger search than college or career. What if it's maternal? Roots and wings. Roots and wings—which will I find?

Chapter 15

"I'm just saying be careful," Dad says. "You never know what you're going to find . . ." He doesn't wrap all of his concern up in the cross-country collegiate issue because he knows there's more. "Have you . . . ?" He uses the two words as though they're a complete question.

Have I . . .

. . . spoken to Jet Blue five times to confirm, switch, then reconfirm my flights?

. . . told Doug and Ula the coffee mavens that I'm taking a break from the café?

. . . thought about where things are going with Charlie? After one long-distance dilemma with Asher, I'm not so keen to keep on with something that's probably supposed to be a summer fling but doesn't feel that way. If I'm at Hadley and he's here during my senior year, it'll be too hard. Should I break it off now? Or is that just cutting a great thing short?

. . . avoided some serious glares from Henry Randall when he stopped by to order a caramel macchiato until his friend Jay slapped his shoulder and told him it's a girlie drink?

. . . considered trying to locate my birth mother, Gala, who could be in L.A.?

Yes to all of the above. But Dad's only real concern is with the college stuff. He's been worried about the Mom stuff before, but often thinks if we don't talk about something, then it's not a problem. So I try to press the issue, just to see if he has any advice or—and this is what I don't want to hear—warnings.

"Have I thought about what?" I ask.

"Nothing."

I know him too well. Just when he might reveal the tiniest bit of info about my mother, he pulls back. "Dad, it's just a quick trip out West."

"You sound so cavalier."

"Like every other Hadley student." He and I have talked and laughed before about how so many prep school students throw around vacation hot spots or travel plans as though a journey to Capri is like a quick trip to the mall.

"But you're not like that," Dad says, defending me to myself.

I sigh and stick my feet into the sink. I'm sitting on the kitchen counter, eating pretzel sticks dipped into cheese that Louisa, Dad's girlfriend, had delivered by next-day refrigerated mail both because she knows I like it and—this is my suspicion— she knows I'm a little annoyed that she's influencing my dad about where I should go to college. Namely, nowhere West. "Oh yeah? How am I?"

"You're down to earth and grateful and . . ."

"Dad?" I stick my toe into the faucet and feel the drops of

cold water run down my foot. "I'm not really changing all that much."

I mean what I say. It's not like I'm a different person than I was last year or even last month. But with each day that fades into the next, there's this gradual shift. And it's not just tastes in music or jeans or even my life dreams or goals. It's more that if I back up and look at myself from a distance, like I do sometimes with a movie camera image or if I'm writing in my journal, there's growth. Not life-altering used-to-live-in-a-yurt-and-now-I-live-in-a-big-city change—more like this feeling I have of everything leading somewhere. How all my actions are connected to the next ones, and all my decisions now actually matter, as say compared to seventh grade or winter of sophomore year, which all feel very episodic. And I want to explain my tangential revelations to my father, to tell him that these days feel profound, but I suspect he'd come back with a "you're just growing up" or worse, not say anything at all for fear he'll—in his mind—lose me further.

"Well, didn't you tell me when you first started Hadley that the more things change the more they stay the same?"

I don't know what he means by this so I just respond with, "It's an old saying, right?"

"Right." Dad clears his throat and sighs. "So, you're off then?"

I swing my feet around from their icy position in the metal sink to the floor, where I've conveniently dropped a dish towel to use as a bath mat. Once I drop down onto the floor, I slide across the linoleum and wood on the towel, faux-surfing until I get to Arabella's room, where I begin to search for a suitable Fourth of July outfit. I agreed to go with her to the Randalls' big party, but since I didn't bring many black-tie gowns (read: I don't own any) to the island, I need to borrow or buy (read: no money, not going to happen).

"I'm not exactly running out the door as we speak but, yeah, I guess my departure is imminent." I say that last part with an English accent as though that will soften the reality.

"Can I give you a little advice?" Dad asks.

"Sure!" I say, the exclamation point nearly visible I'm so glad he has something to offer other than dismay at my Stanford interview and the morph into adulthood.

"Okay, before you meet with Martha Wade—and remember, she's a Hadley trustee, so I know her quite well by now—you should brush up on your college questions: What did she study there? What your own interests are, how Hadley Hall in particular set you on a path to Stanford. Usually alumni interviews are done locally, so she's really going out of her way to meet you . . . there." He pauses before *there* to slip in his feelings about that location.

"Got it. Brush up on facts. Anything else?"

"Oh, it's tricky, Love. I want you to do the best you can—and I can't believe you're old enough to go off on a college interview. Not to mention all the way across . . ."

"Dad, it's not the first time I've traveled by myself."

"All I'm saying is that I don't know what's at the end of . . . whatever you'd call it. A scavenger hunt?"

"Hmm, scavenger hunt is when you have to pick up things like pinecones or photos with the Red Sox mascot, Wally. I think it's a treasure hunt."

"Well," Dad says, and I can envision him shifting from one foot to the other, roughing his stubble and worrying. "What's the treasure?"

I pause in Arabella's doorway, looking at the mess in front of me. Unlike her usual tidy self (her room at Bracker's Common was an ode to neatness, her flat in London always in order, same thing with her room at Hadley), the bedroom looks like all of the items got together in a blender switched on with no top. Read: books, bathing suits, sarongs, prairie skirts, miniskirts, shorts, cutoffs, flip-flops, sandals, running shoes (not that she likes to go running with me on a regular basis, but every once in a while I can convince her), CDs, and various knitting projects are scattered on every surface—bed, night table, floor, and layered on chairbacks and the floor lamp.

"The treasure?" I ask amidst so many items that were probably—when originally purchased—considered treasures in their own rights. "I don't know."

"Oh," Dad says, "I didn't know if you had an idea of what—or whom . . ." He lets his words fade and I know what he's thinking. He's thinking it's my mother, his ex, the one he hasn't seen in almost two decades and the one I've never met. And I want to tell him he's wrong, that the journey Mable set me on has nothing to do with her. But I can't say that, because part of me suspects that it's true.

"Whatever it is, Dad, it'll be okay," I say.

"I'm nodding even though you can't see me," he says. "I love you and . . . just do your best and be . . . happy."

"I'll try. And you have fun, too." I'm about to add something silly about eating sardines in Sardinia, where he and Louisa are headed for their holiday, but I notice something in Arabella's heap that gives me pause.

"Bye, Love," Dad says. "And I almost forgot. Two things: Poppy Massa-Tonclair turned in her final evaluation of your journal project . . ."

"Really? Oh, my God—what'd she say?"

"I'll send it to you. But the gist was that she thinks you've got promise!" He's clearly thrilled for me, and my heart races with the news. My emotions soar to a new pinnacle of excitement.

Then he adds, "And you got your dorm assignment. You'll be in Fruckner House."

From pinnacle to pit of despair. "What?" I snap out of my revelry. "There's no way I can live there . . ."

"It's all rebuilt," Dad assures me. "After the fire they really outdid themselves with the renovations. It's far beyond any of the other houses—bigger rooms, nicer kitchen . . ."

"Dad, it's Lindsay Parrish's dorm."

Dad tsk-tsks. "Are you girls still not getting along? Well, hopefully that'll change."

"Dad, there is no way in hell that I will ever be friends with her. If I can make it through a day without a sneer from her, let alone a term, it'll be a miracle."

"Well, you have all of senior year to work that out," he says, not understanding in the slightest that boarding sucks, period, boarding in Lindsay Parrish's house where she's the queen, at a school where she's the co-head monitor with my ambiguous amore Jacob—well, that's just intolerable.

We hang up and I'm still in my state of shock when I remember the item on the floor that distracted me in the first place. Underneath Arabella's bed—as if it were shoved under there for safekeeping, or, um, hiding—is a bright yellow bathing suit complete with tiny monogram—HR. I pull the shorts out from under the bed with my toe and examine it from a distance like they have the potential to bite—which maybe they do. Reasonable explanations for my best friend to have Henry's bathing suit within the confines of her bedroom?

1) She borrowed it (unlikely)
2) He visited here and left it after changing and his friends left postchanging items, too (semilikely)
3) He left it here after a private postbeach gathering with Arabella (most likely)

So without getting angry—I mean, it's not like the bathing suit means anything necessarily—I slide the suit back into its cave and consider what I should do. If I tell Arabella I saw it, she'll either come clean with its significance (or lack thereof)

or brush it off as nothing. But if I just allow things to unfold—
as Mable suggested first thing this summer—maybe the truth
will be revealed to me. From the other room, I hear Arabella's
footsteps on the stairs and wonder what she'd do if I just
brought the bathing suit out to show her.

Chapter 16

"Hal-lo?" Arabella's voice booms from the kitchen and I can hear her drop her sunglasses and bag on the counter. It's funny how you get to know the music of someone's actions. I know the way my dad's shoes sound in different seasons, his happy walk, his sad whistles—and I know the same things about Arabella. She's in a good mood, I can tell, from the easy way the keys, glasses, and bag clinked down. If she were annoyed, she'd have clomped them onto the counter.

"I'm in here," I say and make sure the yellow suit is back where it belongs. "I'm searching high and low for an outfit." High and low, high and low, like Mable's clue. California beckons and I'm so curious about what's out there. What if I get to Stanford and find it's exactly the school I want? Or what if I land and want to turn around before I've stepped foot outside of the airport?

"Be right in," she yells, and then I can hear her mumbling—presumably into her phone, though possibly to herself.

"That was Chris," she says, explaining the mumbles.

"How's he doing?"

Distracted, she shrugs. "Fine. Now, what about this?" From the far left side of her closet, she pulls out a hot-pink dress that's short in the front and long in the back.

"Um, are you forgetting that I'm a redhead?" I hold up my pile of auburn locks next to the dress. "Next!"

We sort through piles of clothing, holding up items for inspection, and then Arabella flops onto her bed. I want to be more excited about this process, about being girly and finding clothing for the Fourth, but I'm not into it. Part of me wants only to go to Charlie's house and meet his parents and see his home life—even if he's been out of it for a while. He's such a secretive person—or maybe not secretive but cautious—that I feel kind of privileged to be let in. And I don't want to miss my chance. But the other part of me wants to . . .

"Where *are* you?" Arabella asks, her arms akimbo.

"California," I say.

She looks away. "Oh. If you're already gone, maybe you should just go?"

"Meaning what, exactly?" I ask.

"Just that you could go now. It's a flexible ticket, right? There's no point in being here if you're just treading water until . . ."

I talk over her to prove my vehemence. "I'm not treading water. I'm swimming. I'm here. I was just thinking about it. Never mind. I'll be there soon enough. What's the difference between now and five days from now?"

"Five days."

I sigh. "I'm getting a soda—want one?"

"You never drink soda," she says.

"I know. I have the sudden urge for orange soda, though."
I slide my feet along the wood floors to the kitchen, wondering if I should ask about Henry's bathing suit's presence in Arabella's bedroom, if I should be a spur-of-the-moment person and just suddenly fly to California, or if I should even tell Arabella that I have no interest in going to Henry's party—that if I go to a Fourth of July celebration, I would ideally celebrate with Charlie, too.

I open the fridge and grab a cold glass bottle of orange soda, then look around for a bottle opener for the top. It's from a local distributor and not the bottle cap you can just twist off. As I look, Arabella's cell phone rings from the counter. I look at the caller ID and see Henry's name.

"It's Henry," I shout to Arabella. I can hear the bed squeak as she stands up in the bedroom.

"Just neg it," she yells.

I press End and the phone is quiet. Then, out of instinct, I press the Send button to see her call list—and find that Chris's number is nowhere to be found. The Hadley area code is different from the Vineyard's—and the last three calls on her phone have been from Henry. I'm just closing her phone when Arabella emerges from her room.

"What were you doing?" she asks.

"Nothing," I say and swallow air, nervous. "Have you seen the bottle opener?"

"Why were you looking at my phone?"

"No reason," I say, even though we both know I'm not

being truthful. Arabella walks away toward her room—her pissed-off walk, with her feet pounding the floor—and comes back with the bottle opener in her hand.

"What was this doing in your bedroom?" I ask, smirking. "No—wait—I don't want to know." I mean it as a joke, but it comes off kind of judgmental. When Arabella just stares at me, I open my soda, swig, and then just proceed without caution. "Why wouldn't you just say you were talking to Henry? Why lie and say it was Chris?"

Now it's her turn to blush and stammer. "I just . . . it wasn't . . ."

"You just didn't want me to be suspicious?"

"Suspicious of what?" she asks. Her *whats* always sound like *fwaht,* so elegant.

My mouth burns with the sweet sting of my drink. "You tell me. If you say suspicious, probably there's a reason."

Arabella backs up until she's seated on an orange and blue faded surfboard love seat. "Okay."

"Okay, what?"

Arabella points to the boogie board chair next to her. "Come sit and let's spill it."

I gulp, place my bottle on the counter next to the infamous cell phone, and sit. "You're with Henry?"

Arabella purses her lips and nods. "Yeah."

I get chills, even though this shouldn't be shocking. Even if it makes sense, when friends hook up, it still feels weird. "For how long?"

"Since before you got here."

Now I'm kind of annoyed. "For that long? You didn't tell me?" I think back to getting here, to hanging out together, to Henry being all flirty with me and Arabella not saying anything. "I . . . you . . . he . . ." Pronouns come sputtering out of my mouth, but nothing follows.

"I don't know, Love. I thought it was one thing—just a quick fling or friends with . . . but I think I really like him."

"So why did you do all that—like send me to his stupid dinner party all dressed up when you were the one who should've gone?"

Her hair twirled around her finger—one of her nervous habits—Arabella answers without looking directly at me. "Maybe I was sort of playing hard to get?"

"So I was the pawn in your little chess drama?"

"No—no—not like that . . . I wanted you to go and have fun, not just so I . . . that I didn't . . ."

It all clicks in. "So when people said that Henry was getting together with some girl on the lawn of the club way after the party ended, that was you?"

"You make it sound tawdry."

I look at her with my antibullshit look. "I think rolling around on the formal grounds of a private club qualifies as tawdry."

"Now you're judging me? This from the girl who hooks up with a summer guy only to ditch her best friend?"

"First of all, I didn't ditch you," I say. "And second of all, Charlie's not a summer guy. He's . . ."

"What is he?" Arabella brings her knees to her chest and tucks herself into a ball.

I pause, looking out the window as though the answer might appear to me in sky writing. "I don't know."

"So . . ."

"So," I say. "What do we do to make all this better?"

Arabella shrugs, her hair shifting with the movement of her shoulders. "I like Henry a lot."

"And does he . . . ?"

"Feel the same way?" she asks, her eyes filling up with tears. "I don't know." I sit next to her so I can comfort her, which is a funny thing to do after we've been so annoyed with each other, but there are so many emotions in one small apartment that we're both overwhelmed. "He was here . . . when you were out the other night. With Charlie. And we . . ."

"You mean late? After I closed up?" I think about how I made the choice to go have dessert at the lighthouse with Charlie and that at that same time, Arabella was with Henry here and how maybe if I'd stayed here, she wouldn't have done whatever she did with him that's now making her cry.

"I'm not like this. I'm that girl that just does what she wants, right?" Arabella asks. But it's not how I see her, honestly. She dated Toby—a charismatic but self-centered guy—who cheated on her, but whom she was prepared to take back. I would never say her self-esteem needs inflating, but at the same time, she's pretty tolerant of guys who treat her poorly.

"What does Henry say?"

"Not much, actually. I don't know if he's off having—being with other people while he's with me—or if he's more into me than he'll let on. He's kind of a closed book."

"Which is funny, because he seems so face value," I say and put my arm around her shoulder. I don't want to think about the back rub he gave me at the beach, about how he flirts with everyone—or more specifically me—although lately he's been pretty standoffish. "He's been kind of rude to me."

Arabella nods. "I think—and I hope you don't take this the wrong way—but I think he's disappointed that you're with Charlie."

"And that's why he's being a jerk?"

"That, plus . . ." She pauses.

"What?" I sigh. When did summer get so loaded with drama and issues?

"He found out your real age—that you've been lying about being at college at Brown."

"And let me guess, you didn't want to cover for me?" I bite my lip and shake my head.

"You know that if it were something important I would. But it seemed so trivial—so dumb. At this point the only reason you weren't coming clean was because of your pride. And I didn't want to lie to him in case . . ."

I know where she's headed—to the female land of thinking way too far ahead. Like if their relationship continues past the summer, becomes some big deal, then she won't have a lie contaminating the purity of their love. "Don't you think you're getting ahead of yourself?"

"Probably," she says, not mad that I suggested it, more agreeing. "Aren't you?"

I think about Charlie, about how it feels to be wrapped in his arms, to talk with him about books, and writing, all while shucking corn and skipping rocks into the water by his cottage, about how I wish he'd say something about the future of this.

"Mable once told me to judge a guy not by what he says but by what he does," I say. "So if I look at Charlie—and granted it's been only a few weeks—it looks promising."

Arabella stands up and silences her ringing phone yet again. "So what're we going to do about the Fourth of July predicament?" she asks.

Suddenly, I get an idea. "I know what to do!" I smile and rush over to her.

"What? What?" Arabella's curiosity is outweighed by my excitement. I pull her over to the door and down the stairs toward the café. She clings to my hand, laughing and along for the ride.

Doug and Ula, the brother-sister coffee team, are whipping the college student slackers into shape, showing them how to better serve the coffee consumers.

"Excuse me, Doug?" I ask and tap him on the shoulder. He's the nicer of the two, so I figure I'll go to him first. Arabella stands by my side, knowing nothing of what I'm about to do. "Doug? I know you're in the middle of something . . ."

"Yes, we're doing a promotion for the Fourth, really trying

to push our new berry-burst drink. It kind of plays to the idea of fireworks, don't you think?"

"Um, sure," I say and then get to my point. "Doug? As you know, I've requested time off next week for my college interviews . . . and well, I wanted to let you know that I'm actually leaving tomorrow. Morning."

Arabella's eyebrows are raised as high as they'll go as she listens to my uncharacteristically spontaneous choice. "And also, Arabella's coming with me."

"I am?" she blurts and then says, "I am!"

Instead of yelling, which I bet Ula would have done, Doug nods, taking it in. He doesn't argue, but says, "I figured something like this would happen. Luckily, we have extra staff for the holiday and, well, I can't say it isn't annoying. And bad business." He looks at me to see if I'll change my mind. Arabella bounces all excited and surprised.

"My aunt planned the trip," I say, even though he knows this.

"I know she did." Doug sighs. "When you get back, you'll need to pick up some extra shifts—just to balance it out." I nod and Arabella follows my lead, being as agreeable as possible. He can't really stop us, but we don't want to leave on bad terms, either. He gives us the go-ahead to leave, but then stops me on my way out. "There is one thing you could do."

"Sure, what is it?"

"You could find a new name for the café. We all agree on that now, right? Something simple, something catchy?"

"We can work on that," Arabella says, suddenly businesslike.

She's been pretty driven this summer, and I imagine she's psyched to get away, to relax from the stress of the job, not to mention the stress of our supposedly mellow summer loves.

"Yeah," I add, my eyes wide, a big grin taking over my face. "We can work on that on the plane!"

And once that's agreed upon, we walk quickly and quietly up the stairs until we're out of earshot of the café. Once we're in the apartment, we let loose and scream, jumping up and down.

"We're going to California together!" Arabella says and squeezes my hands.

"I know!" I say back, the adrenaline making me shaky. "Let's pack!"

And suddenly, the trip that seemed overwhelming seems fun and filled with potential. And the parties and guys that were tearing at my friendship don't seem to tug at me as much. Of course, I'll have to tell Charlie that I won't be around for the holiday. But maybe a little distance will do as the expression suggests and make the heart grow fonder. Or, if it's not meant to be, make the desire fade out. Either way, I'll miss his big declaration at his parents' house, but whatever it is can't compare to heading West with my best friend, to interviewing, to partying with the stars, to looking up my past—and maybe finding the woman responsible for putting me on the earth in the first place.

"Let's get ready," Arabella says and thrusts a suitcase at me.

I watch her fold shirts and shorts, watch her slide her passport into her bag—she brings it everywhere with her—and answer, "I already am."

Chapter 17

"Read me the list again?"

"Wait, first I need some licorice." I bought an industrial-sized bag of chocolate Twizzlers, one of the best candies on the face of the planet, and we've been eating them the whole way across the country.

"Vineyard Café, Vineyard Brews, Joe 'n' me . . ." Arabella points to each idea with her pen.

"Wait—stop there. Cross that off. I can't stand the word *Joe* for *coffee,* and the grammar is totally wrong."

"Picky, picky. Okay, continuing: Daily Grind, S2G2—I know that's short for Slave to the Grind Two, but it sounds like a robot. Anyway, how about Drip Drop?"

"How about not?" I say and thwack Arabella with my licorice. We have a brief candy duel, and then I look out the tiny airplane window to see where we are—still above the clouds, the land out of sight below us.

"We still have an hour to go. Just focus on this and stop fidgeting," Arabella says. "Another one we came up with was Edgartown Espresso."

I wrinkle my nose and Arabella copies me. "Why can't I think of something good? I feel like since I admitted to myself that being a writer might be the next plan of action for me, my words have stopped flowing."

"I know you'll think of a great name. You just need to close your eyes and think of it." In fact, I'm going to close my eyes right now . . ." Arabella settles peacefully into her seat while I flip through the trashy magazines she bought for the trip and wonder about the renaming. Nothing coffee-esque. Just a simple idea—one that welcomes you without having to lure you with espresso or latte or whatever fad drink might be in that year.

"Bels," I say. "Bels." I elbow her, and she opens a sleepy eye. "I got it." She waits for me to announce it. "Mable's. Just Mable's."

"See?" she says softly, closing her eyes again. "You *are* a writer."

I don't say anything back. I just look out the window at the padded sky, each cloud illuminated, and wonder if she's right— if I will write, or if it's like singing, and it will fade or morph into another interest. In my pocket is my ticket stub, something I'll save and write about—a marker of where I've been and with whom and why. My life's map. And where does all this fit into the map of my life? What will college interviews and London and Charlie and Mable's search lead to?

And then I remember Mable's instructions as to what to do next. *Get on board.* Maybe she means my clue is onboard— that'd be obvious. I check my seat pocket for a letter, then realize she'd never be able to get a letter in there without some big-time strings. Not even the cabin attendant has a clue for me. I'm stumped. But maybe, like my visit to the used bookstore in town where I thought I'd find a clue but instead found an original Poppy Massa-Tonclair novel, I'm supposed to look in the wrong places.

"What do you think she means?" I ask Arabella as we study the luggage journeying around in circles waiting to be reclaimed.

"I thought it meant onboard the plane," she says and coils her hair up into a knot and slides gloss onto her lips. So tanned and summery, she looks like a native. I meanwhile am rosy-cheeked, my red hair has threatened to turn into the bright copper of a new penny, and unless I get a clue about the clue, we're going to be hanging out here all night long. My phone alerts me to messages of which I have two—one from my father, telling me to call him, and one from Charlie, saying he misses me already, which of course makes me grin inanely and forget to call my dad.

"Screw it. Let's just rent a car," Arabella says, ever the problem solver, especially where money's no issue.

"A) I don't have the money for that and b) you have to be twenty-five or something to rent a car."

Arabella squats down, exhausted from travel and the big burst of energy we had right before leaving the island. She never phoned Henry to tell him of her whereabouts, and I spoke to Charlie only briefly, telling him I was off to the palm tree state and he'd have to tell me his big surprise when I get back. He was actually happy I made the decision to go, as if my sudden spontaneity makes me a more freewheeling person—which I guess it does, albeit under slightly false pretenses.

I take out a piece of paper and scribble *onboard* onto it.

"What're you doing?" Arabella asks.

"Trying to see if by looking at the words they suggest anything—an answer."

"You mean if you rearrange the letters?" She takes the paper from me and turns it around. "I haven't got a clue."

"Maybe we should just start shouting 'get onboard' and see what happens," I say. "I'm joking, of course. Doesn't that make you think of the Stage Rage class at LADAM?"

"Yeah, but maybe you're onto something. What if we just walked around and looked for clues, people or . . ."

"Or maybe—maybe . . . Just come with me." We sling our bags onto our shoulders and walk together to the information desk, where I ask, "Do you have a phone book?"

The info lady hefts a giant book onto the counter and, despite Arabella's protests, I begin to page through the book, looking up any stores that could be called Get Onboard.

"You're a raving lunatic, you realize?" she asks, leaning her head on her hand and watching me use my finger to point to all the names that could or could not mean anything.

"Look, I'm trying, okay? Where the hell else are we supposed to go? My interview isn't for days; we have no hotel, I, at least, have no money, and we're too young to get a car. So. Any better ideas?"

Arabella pauses for a moment, eyeing me, and then, drama

girl that she is, puts on her most proper English accent and turns to the information woman. "Terribly sorry to bother you, but I wonder if you could help?"

"That's why I'm here," the helper says.

"If I say the words *get onboard* to you, what does that mean?" Arabella smiles at me, haughty and proud of her simple solution.

But the info lady looks completely blank. "Get onboard the plane?"

Arabella slumps, acquiescing. "Fine, I have no idea."

"Get onboard—never heard of it," the information lady says as if we've purposefully picked something about which she has no information and are therefore evil.

"Get onboard?" says the guy standing to the left of us, waiting his turn for information. He's barefoot, with sunbleached hair and shades, his T-shirt wet. If I didn't have Charlie waiting back East (at least I think he's waiting . . .) I'd be drooling. Okay, so I'm still a little drooly. Just because you eye other people doesn't mean you're less in love, right? Am I in love or only in like? Or neither—and why the need to classify my feelings?

"Yeah, get onboard," Arabella says slowly to the guy. "Does that mean anything to you?"

"Sure," he says and slides his sunglasses to the top of his head. "Get on Board—the surf shop on PCH—near Malibu."

I look at Arabella and she looks at me, and both of us shrug simultaneously. "Want to try it?" I ask her.

"We don't have much to lose, right?" Arabella says, pulling her long-sleeved green T-shirt off to reveal a bright white tank top underneath. Against her skin, it nearly glows. I poke in my bag for anything resembling fashion and grab a navy T-shirt.

"I'll change in the car," I say.

"What car?" Arabella wants to know, and I point to the taxi sign with my pale finger and we lug our stuff and join the line.

Chapter 18

In the taxi, I crouch down so I can whip my current plane-gross T-shirt off and slide into the navy shirt I pulled from my bag. While I'm face to knees, I ruffle my hair to get it to stop clinging to my scalp and do a massive flip, hitting Arabella in the face with the ends.

"Ouch," she says and peels my hair from her eyes while eyeing me. "Better, though. You and your straight hair." She plays with her tousled mop and hands me Chap Stick so I don't get too parched.

"You realize, of course, that I have no way to pay for this," I say and nervously watch the meter click as the fare increases.

"Didn't you save your tip money?" She pats her pocket like the contents of the Slave to the Grind (hopefully soon-to-be-renamed-Mable's) tip jar are all in the confines of her shorts.

"Yeah, but it's in the bank. And it's supposed to stay there." I sigh and look out the window. The taxi follows the curves of the Pacific Coast Highway, and I can't help but be calmed and invigorated by the blue-green water, the soft rush of the wheels on the pavement, the curiosity of what's to come.

"I'll get this one. You get the next one," she says. Arabella's always willing to pay for things or do more than her share—partially because she's just generous, but part of it must come from her large trust fund that kicked in at age fifteen. When there's no shortage of money, I guess it's easy to be free with it. But while I love her for trying, I don't want to feel needy or that I'm taking advantage of her in this way.

"It's not a problem," I say and smile to cover my worry. I open my bag and take out my wallet, holding the bills for an impending stop.

"Okay," the cab driver says from the front. "Here you go. That's Zuma over there and that . . ." He rolls down his window and points to a small building that looks like something out of a surfing movie from the 1950s. "That's Get on Board. My son's big into waves—that's how I know."

He pops the trunk and we collect our bags, totally uncertain if we're in the correct spot, what this all means, or where we're headed.

"Hey," I say as we carry our stuff toward the surf shack whose sign reads GET ON BOARD and then, in sun-faint letters, STAN'S SURF SHOP. "At the very least, we're at Zuma Beach, in the sun, with each other."

"Right." Arabella nods and puts her sunglasses on. "It could be worse. Now, are you going to ask inside, or am I?"

We pass a sign that depicts an image of a surfer bright against a blue background.

"Come pose for a photo," Arabella says.

"Could you be more touristy?" I ask, not embarrassed, but amused, by her. She's half ultrahip and half gawking out-of-towner. "I'll oblige one picture now and then we have to figure out what we're doing here."

She and I stand near the sign, our arms around each other, and do one of those pictures where one of you holds the camera out as far as you can to make it look like someone else took the photo.

Arabella looks at the image on her digital camera. "That sucks. We have to get someone to take it for us." She scouts around and summons some boy from near the front of the surf shack. "Excuse me? Hal-lo? Could you come do us a favor?"

The guy shuffles over in his flip-flops and bathing suit, and when he's closer, appears to be caught off guard by me. Then he shakes his head. "Sure, give me the dig." Arabella hands over the goods, and the guy quickly snaps a picture, all the while looking a mite confused.

"Anything wrong?" I ask because I can't take the scrutiny.

"Nah," he says and turns to go. "I thought you were someone else. But I guess not."

We follow him back toward the shack and climb the two steps up the porch so we're officially inside amidst colorful boards and various people in stages of surf gear. Immediately when I'm inside, a girl comes over and says, "Hey, I was wondering when you'd . . ." Then she backs up and waves her hands around like she's clearing smoke. "Whoa—sorry—wrong person."

"I'm getting a lot of that. It's okay," I say and look at Arabella, who gives me a look.

The girl shouts to someone at the back, "James, check it out. There's a girl who looks just like . . ."

Some guy—probably James—comes out and nods vehemently at me like I'm on display for the surfing populace. "Dude, that's messed up." Then he transfers his gaze to Arabella. "D'you guys need help?"

"Maybe," I say. "Um . . ." And then I'm stuck for words. (It's conceivable that I'd just wander into town and go to Zuma, but less likely that I—who have never surfed—would just show up at the surf shop right from the airport.) But before I can blurble a vague sense of why I'm standing here with my bags and my British friend, another woman comes over and starts to cluck at me.

"Oh my God! It's true. You've got to be . . . Wait. Stay here," she tells me.

I look at Arabella, who shrugs since she doesn't know what the hell's going on either, and then we stand there with the surfing posse gawking at me. The guy who took our picture sees our discomfort and confusion and walks over with a couple of bottles of water. "Here. So I take it you're not from here?"

I shake my head. "No—Boston."

"Ever surf?"

"Nope," I say right as Arabella's saying, "Yup. In Cornwall. England." This starts them off on a conversation about which I know nothing. The guy's been to Cornwall, too, and surfed there, so he and Arabella blather on while I stand there thinking about a potential Plan B and what it should entail. Swimming? Sleeping? Surfing? Without a car and without tons of funds, I'm figuring that sleeping here until my interview sounds about right.

"I'm Chase, by the way," the surfer guy says, and shakes my hand, then lingers on Arabella's. Then he turns back to me. "You must think we're all kind of crazy with the way we're staring at you . . ."

I twist my mouth and nod. "Um, kind of. What's the deal, anyway? I feel like I'm a punch line to a joke I haven't heard."

"She's a writer," Arabella says, thumbing to me so Chase sees. "Just in case you were wondering."

"Got it," Chase says. "She's got that writerly look about her." I listen to them talk about me in the third person and wonder how I made the transition to looking like a writer when I haven't, in fact, published anything except that article for *Music* magazine the summer before junior year. "Look, I think Jess went to find . . . Never mind. What brings you here? Not that I'm sorry to find you lost here—or, are you lost?"

"We don't know what we are," Arabella says and introduces herself.

"We were given—this is going to sound all covert and weird—we were instructed to come here, we think."

Chase looks at us like we're aliens spewing another language. "Okay . . ."

"No, wait. Don't think we're freaks . . ." I try again. "My aunt—her name was Mable, and she sent me on this treasure hunt thing and she told me to get onboard and we . . . I thought it might have something to do with this shop."

Chase nods. "I get it. I think." He thinks for a minute. "Look, I don't think anyone here has anything for you—or, um, that they know what you're doing. But we have another store on the other side of the beach, so we could go there."

Arabella squeezes my hand to say okay. "Can we walk?"

"Sure thing," Chase says. "Just put your bags on the surf-mobile." Said vehicle is outside the shop, an orange car with a caddy attached to hold surfboards and—now—our luggage.

Chase leads us down the length of the sand, past a few food stands, past sunbathers and surfers, bikini-clad girls, and worked-out guys all on display.

"Do you mind if I take a quick detour and grab a hotdog?" Arabella asks.

"I think you have to have a known destination to qualify for a detour," I say but shrug so she knows it's fine. "Mind if I keep going?" I'm itchy to get somewhere—anywhere—on our magical mystery tour before the Fourth of July fever sets in here and no one can help us figure out what to do or where to go.

"Chase?" Arabella asks. "I just walk down the beach, right?"

Chase looks at me with his eyebrows raised as only a guy on the prowl could—to ask if he can stay with my hot British friend. "Just point me in the right direction and I'll see you there." I shift my bag up so the straps stop cutting into my bare shoulders. Note to self: need to apply SPF before I turn a shade of red appropriate only for a crustacean.

Arabella smiles at me, gives me a small thumbs-up, and Chase saunters with her over to one of the food stands. I gaze out at the wide blue sea and keep walking, sand trapping in my flip-flops, then shifting out.

Finally, I'm a few yards away from another Stan's Surf Shack complete with a GET ON BOARD sign out front, which I take to be an omen, and a straggly looking man with bleached-out surfer's hair, who I take to be Stan. Not that I'm psychic or anything—the guy saw me looking at the sign and then him, and pointed to his chest and nodded. Got it.

A few wet surfers sit drying in the sun on the ramp that leads to the sliding door, a couple of girls in boy-cut shorts and tank tops wax their boards, and from the inside a slobbery, shaggy dog pokes its snout out as if to greet me. Maybe the canine holds the clue to all this, I think and decide that since I obviously haven't got a clue about what to do, I should act like a local—that is, mellow out. I drop my bags by the ramp where I can keep an eye on them and then sit my tired butt down on the edge of the ramp, my legs dangling down while I wait for Chase and Arabella.

"Hey." A surfer boy in wraparound dark shades nods at me as he walks the length of the ramp.

"Hi," I say back. At least people are friendly.

"Do you want to . . ." Sunglasses boy stops and then does a double take. "Hey, sorry. Thought you were . . ."

"Let me guess—someone else?" I ask. The guy nods at me. "I've been getting that a lot." It's either annoying or amusing when people mistake you for someone else—but the amount of times the phenomenon has occurred in the last two hours is remarkable. "Who'd you think I was, anyway?"

The guy points a tanned arm toward the darkness of the shack. "See for yourself."

A chill comes over me even though the sun's still out and the air is beyond warm. I slide my legs back up from their dangling position and bite the top of my lip like I always do when I'm nervous. The feelings I have are from nowhere. I mean, why be nervous about this? But something in my gut pulls at me, and I gulp as I walk inside.

Get on Board is set up just like the other one, with a wooden counter off to the right with a cash register and various surfing supplies on offer. If I surfed or had any clue about the sport or activity, I might know the names for the waxes and straps and wet suits, but I don't, so it all looks like a jumble of colors and strings.

Way over to the left, rows of boards lean against the wall, some freestanding, some displayed by hooks on the wall. Despite the number of people outside, the inside is empty. I pause in the cool dim and am almost ready to leave to go wait for Arabella and her man of the moment, Chase, when a raspy female voice shouts from the back room. I can see boxes but nothing else.

"Just a sec. What do you need?" the voice calls out. The young woman has one of those voices that sound like they belong on air—a DJ, a singer, an emcee for an offbeat invitation-only event.

"Nothing," I say because I seriously don't know what to say. "I'm just looking." That part's true—though looking for what is anyone's guess.

"Everyone needs something . . ." the voice says, and I can hear boxes thumping and from the back storage room I see the girl's back as she pulls a big cardboard box toward the wooden counter.

"Do you need help?" I ask, wondering when Arabella will appear. She's probably filled to the brim with hotdogs, soda, fries, and flirting by now.

"I got it," the girl says, and then stands up and turns around so we're face-to-face, maybe five feet apart. Her mouth hangs open. My mouth hangs open. It's not a complete *Parent Trap* moment, but it's damn close.

"Oh, my God," I say.

"Yeah," she agrees. "I'm, like, the blond you." Then she touches her long, straight streaked hair. "Except if I didn't do the highlights, I'd just be you. With different eyes. I knew we must . . ."

"Wait—what?" I steady myself on the wooden counter and the girl comes over so she's standing next to me.

"I'm Sadie," she says and smiles. "You must be Love."

"How do you know?" I ask before I've done the visual

math myself. It's all too surprising and crazy. I stare at her more, trying to take it all in—but I'm too shocked.

"Because I know," she says and turns her head to the side so she's looking me right in the eye. I notice her mouth has the same shape as mine, but her eyes are totally different, brown the color of a chocolate lab. "Because I'm your sister."

Chapter 19

No amount of *Oprah*-watching, no amount of Disney movies or even lottery-type fantasizing can prepare you for meeting a relative you didn't know existed. So I just stand here, in the surf shack, freaking out. My mind flips between being overrun with questions, words, and chatter and being completely void of anything comprehensible.

"So, fine, I'm not your sister—but your half sister," Sadie says and tips her hair over her eyes, either checking for split ends or—more likely—giving herself a shield against the weirdness of the moment. "But half still counts, right?"

I start to talk and my words jumble in my mouth. "Yeah—but—yeah, I just . . ." Does it count? Of course it does, on some level. But I've lived this long as an only child. Don't siblings mean you share toothpaste and fight over the window seat and tell each other things you'd never tell anyone else? Maybe . . .

"It's okay," Sadie says. She's taller than I am, a little bit more broad, but not by much. Aside from the eyes and the fact that she's a redhead gone to the blond side, we're similar. Correction: intensely similar looking.

"No wonder everyone kept looking at me funny," I say. Sadie nods her head, which freaks me out more because it's the way I nod my head, not so much up and down but out and back—Arabella has accused me before of looking like a pigeon when I nod. "I nod like that," I say and don't care if it sounds stupid.

"The pigeon?" Sadie cracks a smile. "My friends always ride me about that . . . Listen, do you want to sit down outside so I can fill you in?"

"Sure," I say and give a half laugh, the still-nervous kind, my hands shaking, my whole body feeling like it's hovering nearby. "That'd be good right about now."

When we leave the darkness of the surf shack and emerge into the bright beach light, Arabella and Chase are making out in broad view by the thatched palapa hut. I cough loudly, but it doesn't stop them.

Sadie cups her hands like a megaphone and yells to Chase. "Hey, Chastity." Then she explains to me, "We call him Chastity because he's just so not." Why does Arabella always seem to wind up with these reputation-heavy guys? Chase and Arabella jump, caught off guard. Sadie waves to them and sits cross-legged on the warm sun-faded wood of the ramp.

"Holy crap," Arabella says, breathy from her short jog over to us. "*Is* this double trouble, or what? Bukowski—you better start explaining." Chase stands there agog, but doesn't speak until Sadie gives him a look.

"I gotta run—but maybe we'll all meet up later? At your place, Sades?" Chase gives a reverse nod and walks off, the question of meeting up or where or when or if we're invited hanging in the air. Your place, your place—her place, I realize, could be Galadriel's—my mother's. Our mother's.

We all lean our backs against the front of the shack and stare out at the ocean as we talk. Maybe it's easier not to make eye contact right now.

"You seem really calm," I say. "I'm not saying that as a criticism, but how can you be so normal about this?" I put my shaking hands on display for her.

Sadie sighs and tucks her hair behind her ears, her T-shirt riding up to reveal deep tan lines on her sides. At least that's something we don't have in common—she clearly got the tanning gene. Then the thought that I share—do I?—genetic info with the person sitting next to me freaks me out all over again.

"Okay, well, the first thing is that I'm kind of a chill person. You know, the surfing mentality." She laughs at herself and then goes on. "Not that this doesn't rank up there with all-time bizarre events in my life. But . . ." She looks at me. Wisely, Arabella is tucked off to the side of us, listening but not intruding. "My mom—our mom . . ."

"Gala?"

Sadie nods. "She told me about you."

"When?"

"When I was young—I don't know."

Part of me wants to skip right there, to Gala and where she is and what she's like and why she left. Then it hits me. If she left me with my dad when I was little and then had Sadie— who's pretty close in age to me—why? Why could she handle one child and not another? What was so wrong with me and my dad and the life she had back in Boston?

"Your face just fell," Sadie says and looks at me with genuine concern.

"Sorry," I say and twist my hair into my fingers out of habit. "It's all pretty big stuff . . ."

Sadie pigeon-nods again. "I'm not going to, like, make up for all the shit that went down with Gala and you and your dad . . . I don't know all the details. But . . ." Sadie breaks her serious tone and smiles at me so sweetly I smile back. She squeezes my hand. "We've met! How cool is that?"

I consider the implications—once you've met someone, you can't unmeet. So now I have a half sister. "I guess it's pretty cool." Then I think about her name. "Sadie . . . as in?"

She nods. "I'll give you one guess."

" 'Sexy Sadie'? The Beatles?"

"Yep—and you? 'All You Need Is Love'?"

"How'd you know?" I ask. "Out of all the Beatles songs with *love* in the titles?"

Sadie stretches her tanned legs out so she can prop her feet up on the railing. "We have that record at home. When I was little I used to look at all the album covers and next to that song, there was a heart in indelible purple marker . . ." She looks at me. "I figured it had something to do with you." Suddenly Sadie stands up and looks at the ocean. "Man, I gotta get in there. One of the reasons I work here is so I can surf and get paid for it. You know, testing boards and stuff. Giving lessons. You want a lesson?"

Finally, Arabella pipes up. "Oh, let's do it! Come on, Love. It'll be fun."

Sadie nods. "The Brit's got a point." Sadie motions for us to follow her inside. "And then later, we'll hang out at my place, okay?" Then she stops. "Oh. I totally forgot to give you this, though." She runs inside, then comes back out with an envelope for me. "Your aunt seemed like a really chill person." She looks at me in silent acknowledgment of Mable's passing. "Sorry."

"Thanks," I say. "You guys get ready and I'll change in a minute. But just to warn you—and, Arabella, you can back me up on this—I am so not gifted in the realm of physical coordination."

"It's true," Arabella says. "Love could fall off a flat surface."

"Whether you fall or fly, it's the ride that counts, right?" Sadie says, then laughs at herself like I would. "Man, don't I do a great surfer-chick?"

Arabella goes to the back of the store through wooden saloon-style doors to change and stores our bags while I sit on a stool and open my envelope.

> Love—
>
> You made it! You gave romance with Charlie another try (I hope), you journeyed to the Vineyard and to California, and you've found Sadie. Whatever—or to whomever—Sadie leads you, I hope you'll stay strong and expand with the experiences. Do you feel I've been along for the ride?

I nod like she's here to see me, and then I start to cry. Not big sobs, but slow tears that sting my cheeks and leave my eyes burning. I assume she means Sadie will lead me to meeting my mother for the first time in my cogent mind. I shiver at the thought and realize it could be mere hours away. Right after attempting to ride the waves. Maybe surfing is an omen, too.

> But like all great trips, this one has to end, too. If I could leave notes for you forever, I would. Then you could be, like, forty and finding notes from me. That'd be pretty neat. Anyway, college looms ahead—and I know you'll pick somewhere that really suits you. It matters, but it doesn't—if that makes sense. It's not an end point. It's another part of your life. Think about where would make you excited and happy—you—not anyone else. Attached you'll find one option. Just one—not the only one. But inside, at least to me, you've always been a storyteller. You're able to set the scene and relay the dialogue so I always feel I'm experiencing everything with you. And I hope you'll keep that going, even though I'm not there to hear it. I love you and always will. Now get out there and live!
> Love, Mable

I fold up her letter and open the other folded paper she has clipped to her note. Photocopied onto white paper is a newspaper article about the Beverly William Award and how Poppy Massa-Tonclair is the judge. All this I knew from my run-in at

the used bookstore in Edgartown, but Mable has used a pink
highlighter to draw my attention to the second-to-last para-
graph, which details the Beverly William Award for Younger
Writers. My heart jumps, bumps, and skips while I read.

> This award, granted to a writer of no more than
> twenty-two years who has yet to publish a book-
> length manuscript, provides publication and a stipend
> to cover one year's worth of living and travel expenses
> in order for the writer to complete a significant por-
> tion of his or her next work. Manuscripts may be fic-
> tion, nonfiction, or creative nonfiction and must be
> turned in by December of the year prior to the award's
> issuing.

Due in December? Right when college apps are due? I sigh,
let down. Like I could ever write an entire book between now
and then while also doing the ridiculous amount of home-
work and college work that needs doing. I reread the info,
memorize the Web site for potential future lookage, and then
tuck Mable's letter and the Beverly William Award paper away
in my bag and flip-flop to the back room to find my half sister (my half *sister*! Holy crap!) and my best friend—and, as
Mable suggested, get out there and live.

Chapter 20

"I could have you practice pop-ups on the beach," Sadie says, her long blond-red hair swaying behind her as she heads right for the water. "But that's way boring. So let's go out to where the waves are breaking . . ."

"Okay," I say, like I have any clue what I'm about to do. "I'm just a lemming. Tell me where to go."

Sadie and Arabella head out into the water and I follow. After the initial shock of being in the water after being hot on land, it feels good to be in the ocean. "I'm trying not to think about *Jaws*," I say and do as Sadie's doing, lying on her board and paddling out farther. I look behind my shoulder at the surf shop, which seems far away and small, the moment of finding out I'm not an only child receding into the past like objects in a rearview mirror.

"Make sure not to hold your board in a position where a wave could knock it back into your face," Arabella says.

"Yeah," Sadie agrees. "Unless you like the broken nose idea. Okay . . . now I'm gonna get you started."

Arabella waits for a wave and seems to effortlessly be carried ashore, popping up on her surfboard on the second try, her sun-lotioned self gleaming in the West Coast rays.

"Put your board here," Sadie says, and puts hers at her side, so I do the same. "Watch the waves that're coming toward you. Then you pick one."

"How do I know which one to pick?" I ask and realize I could be talking about guys or friends or colleges.

"You gotta look and check it out. Find one that's big enough and pick one that will pick you up and take you in but not so big it'll crush you." Sadie grins at me and wipes the wet hair back from her face. In the water, I imagine we look even more alike, with her hair less blond and mine pushed away from my eyes. We tread water there and look at each other. "Go for it."

"I'm scared," I say and know I'm talking about more than finding the right wave. My life is changing a million miles a minute right now. Relatives are popping up and fading, locations are shifting, and my own expectations are unknown.

"I'm right here. Go for it!" Sadie sounds so confident and sure that I'll be fine that I start to believe her.

One big wave passes, then a small one—too small—and then I see one and ask Sadie if she's going to take it. "Yeah, now, watch me." I watch her get ready and she yells her narration to me. "You're on a small, light board, so you're going to have to work a little harder. Right as the wave's about to reach you, push . . ." She's up on the board and yells back. "When you're belly down on top of your board, paddle . . . The wave'll pick you up! You should feel the board rise in the water and . . ."

Then I can't hear anything else and I'm alone in the water. I could think about what lurks underneath me, or what lies ahead with potentially meeting my mother today—or the various thrills and trappings of love, lust, and a long-distance relationship with Charlie (not that Martha's Vineyard to Hadley qualifies as super long distance, but it's enough to matter), but I don't. Instead, I feel my body relax and float in the ocean. I listen to the waves and find myself doing what Mable said I do well—experiencing the moment both so I can tell about it later and live it now.

I pick the wave that feels right to me—not by thinking but just by feeling—and paddle hard, my arms sore but still going, and then, in a big leap of faith, I stand up. Of course, I'm only up for a few seconds or so—with my feet on the surfboard and my arms out for balance, the water gliding under me, propelling me forward to the beach, where Arabella and Sadie are waiting for me.

While Arabella and I change into dry clothes, Sadie walks over to talk to Stan, the owner of the surf shops and to Chase, who's back, to find out what he and their surfer friends are doing later.

"Have you asked yet?" Arabella says, and I don't have to demand clarification.

"I'm too . . . overwhelmed."

"You have to meet her, Love," Arabella says and shakes her hair out like a dog, splattering me with salty water.

"Thanks, Fido," I say. "Of course I want to . . . but I don't want Sadie to think I'm only interested in meeting Gala and not in hanging out with her. I mean, maybe she hasn't brought up Gala because the woman still has no interest in meeting me. Even after all this time."

Even though she has a daughter. One she didn't desert. I try sliding into my jeans but have that post-water tugging experience of having them stick to my thighs. Instead of the denim I go for a casual skirt that makes me think of walking hand in hand on the beach with Charlie. I want to call him and hear his voice—find out what his big announcement is that he plans on saying at his parents' fancy dinner—but I feel like with my news of Sadie, I'd be upstaging him. And with my dad, too. I call Dad's cell to leave a message that I'm here and fine and safe, but I don't add anything else. I don't want him to be all excited about his trip to Europe with Louisa and have me drop the sibling bomb. Unless he already knows. Thinking of life back East reminds me of how fast the summer always goes and then how school slams you with that rush of newness for all of three seconds until you realize it's always going to be the same. Except this year is my last year at boarding school and now I'm in Fruckner—the same house that Lindsay Parrish is in—so the suggestion of things remaining the same is unlikely. For a minute I can transpose myself from the beach in Malibu to the dorms at Hadley Hall, and it's fall or winter and I'm in a sweater rather than a tank top and—and why is it that in these imaginings, Jacob is always there? I have a confrontation with my imagination and remind myself he's hardly at friend level right now, let alone parietal level of visiting me in my as-yet-uninhabited dorm room. But I digress.

"God, you just got your Jacob look," Arabella scolds me.

"I get a look?" I ask, blushing.

"Yes, it's like this." She looks wistfully out the window to the sea and dramatically rests her face on her forearms.

"I'm not that bad," I say. "Am I?"

She shrugs. "So when are you going to ask about your mum—or do I have to do it?"

"I guess I'll ask Sadie when she comes back," I say. "What do I do? Just say, 'How's Gala' or 'Can I meet her,' or what?"

"That's really for you to figure out," Arabella says. She brushes her hair and then we pack up our stuff, balling up the wet bathing suits in a plastic bag. We take our luggage outside and sit on the ramp, our hair drying in the now-fading sunlight. Sunbathers and swimmers are packing up, going home or going out, getting ready for that transition from daytime into evening.

"It's almost the Fourth of July," Arabella says.

"I know. I kind of wish . . ."

Arabella nods. "I know—that you could be with Charlie?"

"Not that it isn't great being here, but I feel badly—like I'm letting him down."

"You aren't. You're just living your own life, too. And of all people, he's got to get that. He's the spokesperson for choosing your own path, right?"

"And what about you and Henry?" I ask and tuck a stray bit of hair behind Arabella's ear.

"Oh, he's just another in my long line of lascivious men . . ." She looks up the beach and sees Chase walking with Sadie. "Maybe I'll find proper distraction here."

"And then what?" I ask. "I spend all this time wondering what my future holds, but you never talk about yours. Are you going for the film or the stage?"

Arabella twists her mouth. "You know, I always thought it'd be film. I can't very well audition for theater in London without everyone blaming nepotism for the casting—or the lack of it. So film would be different."

My eyes widen. "We should so try to get into Martin Eisenstein's party!" I say. "It's tonight, right?"

Arabella claps her hands. "Oh, let's do it! Do you think Sadie'll be into it?"

I debate by tilting my body back and forth like a metronome. "I don't know . . . It might not be her thing . . . Plus, what about meeting Gala?"

Sadie and Chase shuffle up the beach and meet us on the ramp. "Where're you guys staying, anyway?"

Arabella and I look at each other and shrug. "We don't actually know yet."

"Good. Then it's settled. You can stay with me," Sadie says. "Let's go."

On the car ride to Sadie's, she explains where her house is (hers = hers and her parents') and how even though it's nice, all the schools she's applying to this fall are on the East Coast. "True, I love the waves, but I'm kind of ready to jump into something new, you know?"

"I know what you mean," I say. "I'm looking at Stanford." For a second I try to calculate the maternity math, but then I figure Sadie—or Gala—will explain it later.

"Wouldn't that be funny if we traded locations?"

"You could just bum around for a year or two . . ." Chase suggests. He's the constant loafer, all tanned and glowing and perpetually in sunglasses and worn-in T-shirts.

"And become a Stan-abee?" Sadie suggests and shakes her head. "No way." As she drives she explains to me. "Stan was this champion surfer who had some epiphany and opened his two shacks. He basically just lives on the beach and barbeques and bums around."

"It doesn't sound bad," Arabella says.

"Not at all," Chase says. "I figure I can delay college for a year or so before my dad flips out on me. It'll be fun while it lasts."

"So you're set on coming to Cali?" Sadie asks me as we turn down a winding road lined with high hedges.

"No, not set on it." I think about how to explain it. "It's more like coincidence and the fact that my college counselor got me this interview with this alumni person here and it's all high-pressured East Coast prep school craziness."

"But if you had your way, what would you do?"

"You mean if I could snap my fingers and be immediately accepted somewhere?" I snap my fingers as I say it. I remember Mable's advice and close my eyes, trying to picture being on a college campus, but just as I'm attempting to find my four-year future, Sadie swings the car through a huge gate that marks the entryway to—

"Ah, here we are," Sadie announces in a perfect British accent. Arabella raises her eyebrows, impressed. "Magnificent Malibu colony . . . acres of land offset by this European-style villa." Then she cuts the accent and shakes her head. "That's my impression of the annoying Realtor who's trying to sell this hulking place."

As we drive up the wide stone-inlaid path, I'm caught between gawking at the size of the house and asking what Sadie means. I go for the info, figuring the tour of trappings can continue once we're out of the car.

"Is this place for sale?" I ask and climb out, standing with my bag in one hand, my feet in a lame yet jaunty position like Julie Andrews before she goes into the von Trapps' estate in *The Sound of Music*.

"Yup, it's on the market for some obscene amount of money," Sadie says and presses a button that makes the double-sized front door open without a sound. Chase, who has clearly been here before, though who knows in what context, follows Sadie inside and Arabella pauses with me on the stairs.

"Are you coming?" she asks.

My shoes feel cemented to the stone steps. My arms stuck in their previsit position. "She's in there. How can I move?" I ask.

"Like this," Arabella emphasizes, putting one foot in front of the other.

"I can't," I say. "I'm freaking out!"

Chase sticks his surfer head out the door, calling to us. "You guys hitting the road, or what?"

"We'll be right in," Arabella responds, and then to me she says, "Come on."

I take a step and feel my knees shaking. Then my cell phone rings. I slide it from the pocket of my bag and check the number. "It's Dad," I say.

"Oh, check it out. You didn't say 'my dad.' You just said 'Dad.' You're becoming a Euro!"

"Or an affected Hadley Haller." I neg the call and feel a little guilty, but the last thing I can deal with right now is telling my dad where I am and whom I'm about to meet. Then the phone rings again. "He's calling again! It's like he can't understand the concept of waiting for me to—"

"Well, he has left a couple messages, right?" Bels says and motions for me to come inside.

"Okay. Here I go," I say and lug my bags up the steps and through the doorway into my mother's house—and prepare to see where she's been all this time, what she looks like in person, find out why she did what she did, and check out the other side of my life, how it could have—but didn't—turn out.

My tour of the house includes: not one, but two, gourmet kitchens with hand-painted tiles, hallways floored with imported French Baumaniere limestone, the pool with its jet fountains, spa, and glass steam room that looks like it could be the stage for a sexy romp or creepy movie scene, Sadie's bedroom suite, and the lush landscaping with palms, cypress trees, fruit trees, and fountains. Impressive, yes, but what's more interesting is what I learned on said tour.

Sadie's parents are divorcing. Her dad's some business guy who clearly has done well and her mom's—um, my mom's—is taking a break from the record industry. She's also seemingly taking a break from being at home, though Sadie hasn't said this. So every time we go to a new room or building I keep expecting her to introduce me.

"She's burned out," Sadie says and shrugs as she shows me Gala's sound-proofed studio building.

"The view is awesome—in the true sense of the word," I say. In front of us is a huge cliff; its rock side plunges into blue water, with steep steps down to a private beach.

"As opposed to the surfer sense, you mean?" Sadie grins.

"But can I ask you something?"

"Sure," Sadie says as we walk to one of the three infinity pools that seem to connect directly with the horizon. Sadie slips off her shoes and dips her feet into the water. I do the same and we sit there in silence until I ask, "The house is really . . . um, it's really great, but it doesn't seem to have . . ." I can't say it doesn't have character, because that'd be too rude. Even though we're genetically linked, we've only just met and I don't want to offend Sadie.

"Anything in it?" she ventures.

Relief ensues. "Yeah. It's like, there are no pictures and no old drawings from when you were little or even . . ."

"I know," Sadie says, overlapping me like it's totally normal that we click and flow so well. "She took out all the record covers and art and—well, supposedly when you're selling a house you've got to make it devoid of personality."

"Oh. That makes sense, I guess." I lift my feet out of the water and then bring them back into the warmth of it. "It just felt weird . . ."

"It's gotta feel weird on just so many levels, Love," Sadie says. Then she puts her lips together, considering whether to say something. "Can I be honest with you?"

"Sure," I say and feel my pulse jump. Maybe she doesn't live here and she's some psycho liar and breaks into houses that are for sale and has a police record. "Is it bad?"

"That depends . . ." She starts and only stops when my cell phone rings. She peers over at the number and asks, "Are you going to pick up?"

I look and am surprised to find it's not my dad and not Charlie and not Arabella from inside calling to tell me she's using the indoor bowling alley or that she and Chase are plotting tonight's plan for Martin Eisenstein's party.

"I'm so sorry," I say to Sadie. "Let me take this for one second. Stay here, though." I don't want her to leave me in the cool but creepy environs of the empty but stunning yard, and I guess I kind of want her to know what's happening in my life—the rest of my life—so I invite her to eavesdrop. Not that she'd necessarily care, but still . . .

"Hello?" I ask even though I know who's on the other end of the call.

"Love." The familiar voice sends my heart flopping despite my attempts at settling it down. "It's Jacob."

"Hey." My voice sounds relatively normal considering I'm next to my newfound half sister at my never-seen-before mother's house as I talk to the guy whose grip on my heart and mind can't seem to entirely fade.

"What's up?"

"Not much," I say, totally lying or—if you want to spin it in a better way—totally glossing over the facts. "What's up with you?" Inane, inane, inane.

Sadie nudges me and gives me the "who is that?" gesture with her palms out and up. I shrug and then try to think of how I'd describe Jacob. I whisper to her, "That guy friend who you're not supposed to feel anything for but . . ." She nods knowingly.

"Well, here's the deal. I was in—well, you know I was in California, right?" he asks.

"Really?" I ask. "Did I know that?"

"I told you at Crescent Beach, but maybe it was all kind of—"

"Yeah," I say, not wanting to tread over old territory of that morning when I thought he'd make a move and instead introduced me to his Euro-chick. "It's been a pretty crazy summer for me so far, so it must have . . ."

"Um, so—I'm here. Now." His words are choppy, telling me he's nervous.

"You're here?" I half look around and expect to see him pop out of the sculpted bushes—my life is so upside down right now, I wouldn't be that shocked. I step out of the pool and let my feet leave sole marks on the pavement. Maybe somehow that's what we do to people—leave soul marks. *Okay, Love, get out of your head and into the moment.* "So where

are you exactly?" As soon as I ask him, I feel guilty. What if
Charlie were having this same phone conversation with some
girl he used to like and maybe still harbors some feelings for?
I'd feel like crap. So I make the executive decision that I won't
see Jacob, even if he's inside the house or also happens to be
heading to the party tonight. Or—no—I know why he's here.
"You're interviewing at Stanford, right?" I ask. That wouldn't
be bad, if we just happened to look at the same school at the
same time. That's just coincidence. Maybe he got the cheap
flight to LAX, too, like Arabella.

"I already did," Jacob says. "It's a great place."

"Yeah? It seems that way."

"But it's not the right place for me," he says but doesn't say
why. "But so . . . then I got to thinking . . ."

Oh no, here we go. It's never a simple "what's up" phone
call. There's always an underneath. Sadie gives me the time
signal, pointing to her watch and then plucking her clothes.
"We have to get going if we're going to change and head up
to the party," she whisses—a whisper-hiss combo. "I hear that
the security for Eisenstein's gala—heh—can take an hour to
clear."

Sheer testament to the enormity of this day is the fact that
a Hollywood glamfest seems blah in comparison to my life
right now. I nod at Sadie and then say, "I'll be done in a sec,"
loud enough for Jacob to hear. Not because I want him to necessarily know exactly where I am or what I'm doing. I don't
need him to be impressed with the fact that I'm spending the day
before Independence Day being really and truly independent

and going to one of Hollywood's biggest bashes, but I guess I don't want him to think I'm here by myself.

I always felt like I was the one who reached out to him, pulling him from his quiet boy status into the social realm, but the truth is, the tables flipped on me and now he's the Hadley *it* guy and I'm—I'm whatever I am—and there's no clear definition to our friendship.

"Where are you, anyway?" Jacob asks and exhales audibly. I can imagine the air leaving his lips, fanning his hair off his forehead. Then I picture Charlie and his smile, the way he kissed me in the lighthouse, and have one of those cartoon images of them in miniature, each sitting atop one of my shoulders.

"I am—at present—walking around one of those pools that blend seamlessly into the landscape, even though it's completely artificial and man-made. Oops, semiredundant."

"Ah, you're your own best editor," Jacob says. "And where is this pool? In Edgartown or—what's that other place—Katama?" He mispronounces the name.

"It's Katama," I say. "But I'm not in either of those towns. I'm in Malibu."

"California?" Jacob sounds more surprised than he should. Or maybe he's really shocked to find that I indeed have a life and that I, too, can go across the country to look at schools—not that I've been exactly academic here yet. But my interview is in a few days . . .

"Yeah, what's wrong with that?" I ask, and hope my tone is friendly but not flirty. But it might be flirty. Just a little.

"There's absolutely nothing wrong with California as a state—or even as a state of mind. But for my purposes, it poses a definite obstacle . . ."

"Wait, what're you saying?" I ask. And then my cell phone rings again. "Jacob, hang on for one sec, okay? I know it's rude and I think we've even talked about the triage of call-waiting and how annoying it is . . . but . . ."

"Fine, I'll be here," Jacob says as I click over.

"Hey, Charlie! I miss you!" I say before I've even had the chance to think about being overemotive.

"Me, too. I just got back from . . . anyway, what's it like there? Are you an instant surfer babe? Or more the red carpet vixen?"

"Um, let's just say I'm neither—maybe in the middle of both." As we talk, I'm reminded of why I don't want to keep a summer thing going—why long-distance romance inevitably fails, just like it did with me and Asher. Not that one person necessarily betrays the other, but that you lose that daily insight; you wind up explaining your life rather than sharing it. With a jolt I remember Jacob's on the other line. Now I have to choose to whom I want to continue speaking. I can't. Quick pro and con—Charlie is in fact my boyfriend and I miss him and want to hear about his planned announcement to his parents that I'll miss tomorrow night. But Jacob is my friend—plus minus—and he'll be at Hadley in the fall. But his intentions are dubious at best. "Charlie? Hang on a second. Let me get rid of someone on the other line."

Get rid of sounds a little more intense than what I mean

to imply, but I click over to Jacob and find him singing to himself, so sweetly, so softly, that I have to steel myself for hanging up.

"Hey, Jacob, I have to go," I say.

"A better offer on the other line?" he asks, his voice jocular, but potent.

"No, it's not like that," I say, though maybe it is just like that.

"Wait . . ." He heaves a sigh and launches into a quickly spewed speech. "I said I was just going to do this and now I'm . . . I have to go through with it. So, the reason why it's too bad you're on the West Coast is that I'm back on the East Coast."

"You are?" I ask. "No Europe? No multicity tour?"

"No, just here."

"Here being . . . ?" I ask. Arabella waves from inside the enormous wall of windows and her silly dance would make me crack up if I weren't doing double-time on the cell.

"Here being on the Vineyard."

A chill comes over me and I tilt my head up to the darkening sky, looking for answers or clouds or both. "Why are you on the Vineyard?"

"You once told me that life is about priorities, right? And I think I was angry at you a long time ago because you never—or I felt like I wasn't your priority—"

"Hey," I interject, but Jacob cuts me off.

"Can I just finish, please? But then I got distracted and

you . . . were away. And then, after Crescent it was just so obvious to me that . . ."

My phone blips at me, the tone seeming insistent and angry. "Hold on, Jacob. Wait. Hold that thought, seriously." I press the button and find that no one's there, but before I can go back to Jacob, Charlie calls again.

"Look, do you want to talk or what?" he asks.

"Don't be angry. It's just nuts here right now. You wouldn't believe it if I told you . . ."

"Well, I hope you will, tell me I mean . . ." he says.

Jacob is on the other line about to confess something and I feel like I have to get back to that. Arabella and Sadie and Chase are flailing inside, telling me to hurry up so we can go to this party that could result in a laugh or could result in a new career—or at least a voice-over deal like Martin Eisenstein suggested. And my mother could walk into her home at any moment. It's all too much. I balance on a carved stone planter, but my legs bristle against the scratchy leaves.

So this is what I look like from above: a red-haired cookie cutout of myself, lying flat on the dark stone slabs by the pool, flanked by glistening circles of water, and surrounded by mass confusion.

"Love," Charlie says, "I need to tell you something."

"Oh, God, you, too?" The words fly out before I can reel them in.

"Why, who else is making declarations?"

"No one," I say. And then I add, "But you have to hang on

for one more minute." *Click*. "Jacob?" I ask and pray that I don't have one of those sitcom moments where I click over to the wrong person and say their name, which results in shouting and blame or hilarity as the situation escalates.

"Love, I came here—I got on that ferry at Woods Hole and now I'm here and I'm feeling a little like an ass because I clearly should have called, but I had this need, I just . . ." Jacob takes a breath and I inhale the warm evening air waiting for him to finish, feeling light-headed and confused. What if you get what you want but it's at the wrong time? "I like you, Love—and even though we agreed to be just friends I'm admitting here that I feel more than friendly . . ."

"You do?" I say, and I can't help that part of me smiles at this idea. He likes me. Again. Or anew. But he does.

"I just want to be with you and see what happens—can't you just see it? Senior year? The two of us?" His questions linger in the air, sending me reeling and almost forgetting to go back to Charlie. "Come back to the Vineyard."

"I have my interviews and stuff," I say, but it sounds like a lame excuse. I can't tell him that my summer maybe-fling, maybe more is also on that island, nor can I efficiently explain the big news of being out here.

"I'll wait. I'll stay with Haverford or Jon Rutter or Nick Samuels or something."

"They're all on the Vineyard?"

"Half of Hadley is here," Jacob says. "So tell me when you're back, okay? I'm here . . ."

"Okay," I say and click over to Charlie, who rather than singing like Jacob was, is ordering fries. He says, "Make it a double order." Then, for my benefit adds, "Just in case my girlfriend manages to instantaneously come back from California to share them with me."

"I'm your girlfriend?" I ask. I move my legs and the arm not holding my phone to my ear like I'm lying in snow, even though lying on the patio in California is sort of the antithesis. It's not as though I thought I wasn't his girlfriend, but it's always good to hear it mentioned out loud, so that without having that awkward "what are we?" conversation, it's a known entity.

"Aren't you?" Charlie laughs. "I wish you were here. My parents were really looking forward to meeting you."

"Were? They're not anymore?"

"Of course they still are. But I think they had high hopes for their dinner party. The fact that I—their ne'er do well son—is making an appearance . . ."

"Plus bringing his stunning new girlfriend . . ." I add. I don't tack on the *I'm only your girlfriend for now* part because I don't want it to be true.

"Right. So . . . it's only been—what?—a day since I saw you? But it feels like so much longer." He sighs, then crunches on a fry. "You've ruined this clam shack forever, you know. I always think of you and that first time we hung out when I come here. I can see the Chappy ferry now, and it's a perfect late-afternoon moment."

"Sounds nice," I say. What I don't utter is just how much

has changed in the hours since I left Edgartown. "There's a lot going on."

"Ah," Charlie says. "Sounds ominous."

"How so?"

"A lot going on is one of those euphemisms that people use when they're hinting at something else—like I hooked up with someone else or I quit my job or something. Don't you think?"

I nod, my head still on the stone patio. "Yeah. But I didn't mean it to sound like that." I sit up and look out at the ocean; from a distance it seems calm, but I know that if I went closer, I would see the definitions of the big waves, hear the churning sounds, and wonder if that's what I do—stay at a safe distance from things and people.

"Since you're not going to be at the dinner tomorrow—I wanted to kind of fill you in on it . . ."

"Oh, right, your big announcement."

"Hey, Love! Come inside—there's something you've got to see!" Arabella shouts from the back door. She waves me over. "It's important." She puts such an emphasis on the word important that I know it's something to do with my mother—or rather, it could be my mother. There, in person, inside.

"Charlie—I have to go in a minute," I say. "I feel really bad—I'm not trying to belittle your thing."

"Hey, it's not earth shattering or anything, but it does semi-affect you. At least, I hope it does."

His excitement piques my interest and I focus on his words. That is, right up until yet one more phone call comes in. I look to see what number it is—it's not Jacob again, thankfully. Wouldn't want to have to choose again. It's just my dad. Guilt. "Charlie, wait one more second. I am not really this phone obsessed. Seriously."

"Hi, Dad," I say, without giving him a chance to speak. "I can't talk."

"I know you're busy, but this is ridiculous," Dad says, but his voice doesn't sound angry. He sounds funny, different.

"Give me ten minutes and I'll call you back." I hang up and go back to Charlie.

"So." Charlie clears his throat. "I know we just sort of covered the girlfriend thing, which we hadn't really dealt with . . ."

"Yes, I believe we did." Part of me is so happy about this, but part of me isn't. I dread the day that summer ends, and it's all good-byes and plans for meeting up, so I admit my feelings. And they have nothing to do with Jacob. "I think you know how I feel about you. The only thing is . . . how do I say this? I'm not the right person for a long-distance thing."

"So you're superceding my announcement with a breakup?" he asks.

"No. No. Not all at. I just—I've been feeling this way and worried about it, so I wanted to tell you."

"From the safety of mileage."

"Maybe . . ." I say and take a few steps toward the house, where Arabella and Sadie and—who knows—await.

"Well, that's what I'm getting at. Remember the spilled shake incident. At Bartley's this spring?"

"Yeah, I think that day's pretty much in the memory bank

for good." I think of the sweet smell of vanilla frappe, Asher dumping me on the phone, visiting with Mable, how good it felt to see Charlie—even if only briefly. How indelible he is to me.

"I was registering. For classes."

"What?"

"I'm going back to Harvard this fall. It's time." If he's at Harvard and I'm at Hadley, we can basically yell to each other from our dorms. Okay, so it's not that close, but it can't be considered long distance. "I'm really psyched about it."

"How come you didn't tell me before?" I ask. He's so withholding sometimes—it's part of what draws me to him, but part of what makes me leery.

"I didn't have official word until right when you and I were getting together. And I didn't want to cloud things."

"You mean, in case this was one of those summer-fun flings, you wouldn't bring it up?" I suggest. It's slightly tricky, but I can't say I blame him. What if I had just been some girl who kissed him and moved on?

"I guess. But it seems like there's a real—oh, you'd know the word better than I—some word that means future but not future. Do you know what I'm saying?"

"You mean we have real potential?" The sun starts its slow decline, the sky shifting into a multicolored wash of yellows, peaches, and pink.

"That's exactly what I'm saying. Can't you see it? You, me, crunching through the leaves in Harvard Square? You visiting my dorm room . . ." He laughs and I join in.

"Sounds nice," I say.

Both images sound nice. More than nice. Awesome. Great. Life changing. Me and Charlie in the Square, drinking coffee and talking endlessly about books and music and living a college-type social life, which would get me out of the dorms at Hadley. And then, too, I can totally see being with Jacob—maybe first as friends, but then the tensions build and we finally kiss after so long. But just because I can picture both doesn't mean I can experience both—at least not at the same time. But does it mean I don't feel any particular feelings toward either guy? Or am I just confused?

"So when can you come back?" Charlie asks. He's probably too cool to say he's waiting for me—but isn't he?

I think about Sadie in the house and meeting Gala and interviewing here and surfing, and trusting that wave you choose, and wonder what would happen if I didn't go back East. If I just stayed here. Not that I can really figure out how or why that occurred to me, but what if?

"Come inside!" Sadie yells. "You're worse than I am on that thing."

"Sounds like you have to go," Charlie says. "But keep me posted."

"Would you be upset if I didn't come back right away? There might be things I need to check out out here . . ."

"More than just Stanford, you mean?"

"Yeah," I say, trying to peer into the house through the windows. "More than that."

"There's no expiration date on my feelings, if that's what you mean."

"I like the way you said that," I say to him.

"Good," he says. "You can put it in a book someday."

Yeah, right, that novel I'm just waiting to pen. Sign me up for the Beverly William Award for Younger Writers. Or don't. I mentally thank Mable for her thoughts about that, but shake my head at the idea of actually doing it—writing a book. Who writes a whole book? Then I say this to Charlie, "Who writes a whole book?"

"A writer," he says. "Like you. Miss you." He hangs up and I'm standing outside, growing a little cold—not so much from the weather as from the idea of what lies on the other side of this door. I grasp the brass handle and start to turn it when my cell phone rings again.

"Dad—hi. I was just about to call you." That doesn't count as lying, right? It wouldn't if I admitted it, so I do. "Well, I wanted to call you, but, I don't know, Dad, I'm losing it out here."

"Well, that makes two of us," he says. I stop in my tracks and listen to him. "I wasn't going to bother you. I didn't want to keep calling you, but . . ."

"Are you okay? Is Louisa . . . ?" Maybe he has to make an announcement himself, maybe he's engaged. Or leaving Hadley. Or changed his mind about my living in the dorms. Wishful thinking.

"We're all fine. Are you okay?"

"I am," I start and then sigh. I could cry just from the stress of it all—but it's all good stuff, isn't it?

"Now, I know you have your interview coming up—"

"Dad, please, please don't start about the West Coast colleges. Really, I just can't take any more right now."

Dad pauses, cupping his hand over the mouth of the phone so I can't hear what he's saying. "This isn't about that. I kept asking you to call—why didn't you?"

"I'm sorry. You know I'm not irresponsible. I let you know that I got here but it's only been a day—not even. What could you possibly need to talk about that you called me like six times?"

"Love . . ."

"What?" I ask. I think about my summer so far, the adventure of Mable's clues, where they've led and to whom, the love I think I've found with Charlie even though there's still the temptation of Jacob. Fall is right around the corner—after the Fourth of July, summer always speeds by—and what will happen then?

"You should probably skip your interview," Dad says, his voice serious.

"Why? So I can choose a school that's close to you?"

"No," Dad answers, not challenging me, just sounding matter-of-fact. "Because you don't have any real interest in it."

This sentence hits me with the weight of a wave crashing on me. Of course I have interest. Don't I? The answer, I realize, standing on my mother's about-to-be-sold chiseled stone steps, is that I don't actually. I wanted to have a valid reason for coming out here, for going to the party, which now seems insignificant, for possibly finding Gala.

In a small voice I tell him, "You're right. But I'm not giving in. If I like a school out here or in Arizona or Europe, I still want the option of looking."

"I think," Dad says, "that I was only keeping you away from the idea of long distance to make myself feel better about you leaving."

I can hear him getting teary, which makes me teary, even though the moment's not really sad. Why is he so sad, aside from still mourning Mable? Is it because I'm headed toward senior year? Or something else?

"I'm not leaving yet," I say. "Unless you count the dorms. Wait. Don't go there right now."

"Maybe it's more like emotional leaving," Dad suggests.

"So why do I need to skip Stanford?" I ask. From an upstairs window, a knocking. I look up and see Arabella and Sadie. All along, I haven't been an only child. How weird. And how cool. And how complicated. Just like love—like life, I guess.

"You've got people here waiting for you," Dad says.

"Did you see Jacob?" I ask.

"We were on the same ferry. Apparently, he came a long way to see you."

"I know. But it's . . ."

"Complicated? I can understand that."

It's so comforting to hear my dad's voice, to have a normal

nonarguing conversation with him. "So why are you there? Aren't you supposed to be on your way to Sardinia or something?"

"We're supposed to *be* there," Dad answers. "But . . ."

With my dad on the phone for support, I open the door and step inside the well-lit living room. Even devoid of personal pictures and personality, it's gorgeous, with vaulted ceilings and a cavernous fireplace (which I'm sure is really useful during the California winters). But no people. Everyone's upstairs, I guess.

"Dad," I say, trying to be honest and close with him. "I need to tell you where *I* am."

"As long as you're safe, it's okay," he says, maybe alluding to the fact that he knows.

"I'm at her house," I say, nervous as hell.

"Really?" Dad says and laughs a little.

"Why is that funny?" I ask, but laugh a little, too. "Just because it's surreal?"

"Life is just so strange. You think it will all make sense when you get older. But it just doesn't. We never even got to the airport . . ."

I remember singing as therapy at Hadley. One song I always liked was "Anticipation," that feeling of what might—not will— but could be. And if this moment were a photograph, that would be the title. I think about singing and then about writing, about how life is one long story with smaller, intricately plotted stories scattered into the longer arc. Will I ever write a novel? And what about my Jacob versus Charlie conundrum?

They're both back on Martha's Vineyard, waiting. And I'm waiting, too. To choose a school, a guy, catch up with my long-missing past, and maybe bring it, or at least Sadie, into my future. It's all potential, right?

"Love," Dad says. "Are you there?"

"I'm here," I say.

"Well, are you coming back?"

From upstairs comes giggling and clomping into the kitchen, which backs onto the dining room, which leads to the living room, where I am. Sadie and Arabella and Chase have met up with various familiar-looking young starlets and their friends. I can see one girl, an actress who always does those remakes of Jane Austen's books. But the star power fails to move me.

"I don't know," I say. "I'm not sure why I need to . . ."

"I'm at the cottage," Dad says out of the blue.

"I thought Mable said it was rented all summer—that's why Arabella and I have that apartment."

"It's not rented," he says. "It's owned. And the owner showed up."

I stand in the hollow room, my voice echoing as I speak. "And . . . ?" Suddenly I remember Poppy Massa-Tonclair, world-famous author, and her words of advice to me. She said that conflict and confusion give way to understanding and depth. So maybe all this will lead to more. I just got here and just met Sadie.

"And the owner of the cottage is Gala. Your mother," Dad says.

"She's there?" I ask.

"Yes. Waiting for you."

Sadie is next to me and I don't know how long she's been standing there, but I guess long enough for her to understand what I heard over the phone.

"I'm sorry," Sadie said. "I should have told you that she went there, looking for you. But I wanted to meet you myself—without having her get in the way." She looks sorry and sad, and I nod at her, wondering if we'll stay in touch or just be these half siblings circling the country but never meeting again.

Arabella comes and touches my shoulder. "What's going on?" she asks, but I can't possibly tell her right now.

"Love?" Dad says, and I look at the phone that's been attached to my ear for a long time. He's standing there with her. The thought is mind-boggling. "What are your plans?"

My plans. If only plans had no wrong answer. Or, if only an answer were simple—meeting my mother or staying here with my half sister? Seeing Charlie, seeing Jacob, asking one of them to meet me at the ferry. Figuring out how to get out of living in Fruckner with Lindsay Parrish. Trying to write something to see if I can do it. Actually interviewing and finding a school that wants me, that I want. Who, when, why, where. Like Sadie said, I have to choose a wave, a path to carry me to where I want to go. Choices and waves, people and past. I imagine it all as an ocean, huge and daunting, soothing and timeless. Which path—what or whom—is next? I have to ride from this moment to the next, all the while wondering where this wave will take me.

Want more?

Summer's lingering a little longer, leaving Love to deal with more than she ever thought she could handle. With September fast approaching, Love has college, romance, and parental issues to sort through—not to mention some things, and people, from her past that won't stay hidden. Love's tough, though, and determined to make good decisions (which boy? which school? which path?), staying true to herself and realizing that every once in a while, what you wish for isn't what you want in the long run. Smooth sailing—even in the form of finding long-lost relatives, or even figuring out what true love is—takes time, humor, patience, and a . . .

Labor of Love

Coming September 2007

Preorder now at **Amazon.com**
and stay in touch with Love
at **www.emilyfranklin.com**.

About the Author

Emily Franklin is the author of *The Principles of Love* series, as well as two novels, *The Girl's Almanac* and *Liner Notes*. Another novel for young adults, *The Other Half of Me*, will be published in August 2007. Her next series, *Chalet Girls*, is forthcoming in December 2007.